This guy...

Niccolo looked as comfortable as a prowling shark in a tank full of minnows. He was younger than she had expected, midthirties perhaps, and his face was the perfect blend of beauty and power.

In all respects, the man was breathtaking.

Apprehension threaded through Sophie and her breathing quickened.

She felt faint as she saw all her hopes of some kind of breathing space fly through the window.

"Who are you?"

Sophie blinked.

"Sophie Baxter." She held out her hand and wondered how she could phrase the beginning of her excuse for backing out of the arrangement his aunt had made. "Your aunt? Evalina? She recommended me to you about the...er...vacancy for the nanny job to replace her now that she's had to return to Italy? I'm really sorry about your father, by the way. It must be worrying for you, stuck over here when you know he's been in an accident..."

"You're the woman my aunt has recommended?"

Cathy Williams can remember reading Harlequin books as a teenager, and now that she is writing them, she remains an avid fan. For her, there is nothing like creating romantic stories and engaging plots, and each and every book is a new adventure. Cathy lives in London, and her three daughters—Charlotte, Olivia and Emma—have always been, and continue to be, the greatest inspirations in her life.

Books by Cathy Williams

Harlequin Presents

His Secretary's Nine-Month Notice
The Forbidden Cabrera Brother
Desert King's Surprise Love-Child
Consequences of Their Wedding Charade

Once Upon a Temptation

Expecting His Billion-Dollar Scandal

Secrets of the Stowe Family

Forbidden Hawaiian Nights
Promoted to the Italian's Fiancée
Claiming His Cinderella Secretary

Visit the Author Profile page
at Harlequin.com for more titles.

Cathy Williams

—

HIRED BY THE
FORBIDDEN ITALIAN

HARLEQUIN
PRESENTS

HARLEQUIN®
PRESENTS™

Recycling programs
for this product may
not exist in your area.

ISBN-13: 978-1-335-56865-6

Hired by the Forbidden Italian

Harlequin Enterprises ULC
22 Adelaide St. West, 41st Floor
Toronto, Ontario M5H 4E3, Canada
www.Harlequin.com

Printed in U.S.A.

HIRED BY THE
FORBIDDEN ITALIAN

CHAPTER ONE

'I AM SORRY, Nicky, but I have no choice. Your *papa* cannot walk with that leg of his in a *gesso*, or whatever you want to call it. Your *mama* is in a state. She needs me.'

With a mountain of work to get through, a pile of reports to sign off and a delicate, monumental deal which had been months in the making nearing its long-awaited conclusion—not to mention a six-year-old daughter who was about to start her summer holidays—Niccolo Ferri had looked at his aunt two evenings before, as she'd stood there with her suitcase packed and the taxi driver all but blowing his horn in the circular courtyard of his London mansion, with something approaching horror.

Yes, his father *had* had a fall, foolishly swerving through the streets of Rome on a moped Niccolo had warned him not to get, but why on earth did that mean his aunt, here in London, suddenly needed to rush off in the guise of Florence Nightingale? To the best of his knowledge, his aunt had precisely zero medical qualifications.

He had telephoned his mother on a daily basis ever since his father had been sent flying off his moped three days previously, and Anna Ferri had certainly not sounded like a distraught woman in desperate need of her sister's help.

Indeed, she had rejected his offer to have round-the-clock nursing installed in their villa in Tuscany without bothering to hear him out.

So, what had changed in the space of twenty-four hours, necessitating his aunt's hasty and ill-timed departure?

'I need you here,' he had said. 'Annalise begins her summer holidays tomorrow and there's no way I'm going to be able to find someone to stand in at such short notice. I might be able to throw money at an agency, but I doubt they'll be able to conjure up a suitable candidate from thin air.'

'I would not dream of leaving you in the lurch, Nicky.' His aunt's words had oozed with a level of soothing piety that had had every antenna in his body quivering with suspicion. 'I have just the lady for you.'

He had conceded because he'd simply had no choice. He had huge respect and fondness for his aunt, his mother's only sister and a force of nature who had spent years travelling the world. She had descended every so often on their tiny eighth-floor flat, sometimes to stay for weeks at a stretch, bringing with her the tantalising scent of adventure, of possibilities of other lives lived in places that weren't poky flats in rundown estates.

As a child, Niccolo had watched his mother's face light up every time Evalina had wafted through that front door, had watched his father relax, laugh out loud, shed some of the concerns that seemed to dog his daily existence.

Where his parents had led a dutiful life, Evalina had thrown herself into travel with the gusto of someone permanently hellbent on having a good time. She was outgoing, engaging, and with a streetwise sharpness that allowed her to wheedle her way into jobs wherever her wandering feet had happened to take her.

Of course, over time, the stars had faded from his eyes and he had realised that where his parents' lives were reduced and constricted through lack of money, his aunt, likewise, had ended up travelling down the same path even if the scenery on the way had been slightly different. He had watched his father work all the hours under the sun, yet, without the required university degree, never finding the voice to make a case for moving up at the family-owned garage where he worked, where kith and kin counted for far more than innate talent and unexploited brains.

Where the right accent got the plum jobs. As a hard-working immigrant, his father had slaved away for years until, three years previously, his heart had decided that the stress was just a little too much, and it had decided to warn him that a change of direction might be a good idea. The help Niccolo had offered the minute he'd started making serious money—always declined because of pride—had finally been accepted because the stakes had been so much higher.

And while his father had slaved away his mother had done her bit, cleaning other people's houses and, at one point, walking other people's dogs.

They were both humble and had never asked for much, and their reward? They had received precious little.

Were they in love? Yes. Were they happy? Yes— they enjoyed one another's company and relished the small pleasures in life.

Was that enough for him?

A thousand times *no*.

And his aunt? So vivacious, so beautiful in her prime, independent and clever...

Yet eventually, in her late fifties, as her exciting nomadic life had drawn to its inevitable close, where had she been left? Without the degree? The diploma? Without any connections whatsoever?

Where had all that excitement led?

To a life without any sort of security, financial or otherwise.

Watching them all as he'd grown up, Niccolo had

absorbed learning curves he hadn't even been consciously aware of.

Innately gifted academically, he had known what had to be done and he had worked. At eleven, he had been accepted on a scholarship to a prestigious boys' private school and he had seen, over the years, where power and wealth and privilege got a person in life. He had seen how people who had a mere fraction of the talent and sharpness of his own father had prospered because they had had the right education, the right background, found the right foothold, could hold their own and blag their way through situations with confidence.

Not always, of course, but often enough for him to have understood the importance of that ladder that led to those glass ceilings waiting to be broken. By him.

He had recognised that what money and power bought wasn't just the house and the holidays. Money and power bought freedom from insecurity, and that had been instructive because what he had seen in his own home had been insecurity. Love had been there, close family ties had been there, but as far as he was concerned they were blighted by the nagging worry about what tomorrow might bring.

He had determined from an early age that he was never going to have to worry about tomorrows.

He had been sought-after following his stellar career at Oxford, but he had chosen the least promising of the companies headhunting him, the one where he could make the biggest mark because it was failing the fastest, and he had spent three years turning it around. From day one, he had asked for shares and just a fraction of the salary he'd been offered. By the time he left, his shares were worth a fortune and he had then moved to diversify every penny he had made, dipping fingers into pies and taking risks in acquisitions that no one would have dared. But Niccolo had had the Midas touch. Everything had turned to gold, and with that gold he had been in the fortunate position to save his parents, and his aunt, from insecurity and those uncertain and frightening *tomorrows*.

And if he'd made one error of judgement…

He thought of his daughter now and sealed shut that door, because it opened onto memories he had conditioned himself not to revive.

Evalina had told him that she had 'just the lady' for him. Very nice, she had said, very reliable, someone she had met at her allotment. More importantly, she had confided, Annalise had met her a couple of weeks ago when they had been there on the weekend.

'Three Saturdays ago, when you were out with that dark-haired woman with the make-up and the *tette grandi*,' she had expanded, while Niccolo had absently recalled the big-breasted woman in question. Their early trip to the theatre had been followed by the expensive meal and relief when he had left with merely a peck on the cheek because somehow the thought of going where the evening should have taken them could not have been less appealing.

Now that his aunt had disappeared, he was relieved that she had not managed to leave him in quite the lurch he had feared. The lady's being a trusted friend from her allotment, and furthermore one his daughter had met, went some way to compensating, presumably, for a lack of formal qualifications.

He trusted his aunt's judgement implicitly. She had fortuitously slotted into his household when her wandering feet had started protesting at the constant travel five years ago, just when he had needed someone. Left with an infant following the premature death of his wife, Evalina had moved in and taken charge, relishing the joys of helping to raise Annalise, which had filled the void of never having had a child of her own.

He had been immeasurably grateful.

His life had been lived in the fast lane from the very moment he had married and he'd realised within six months that it had been a mistake. No time to press a rewind button and no pause to draw breath and take stock. Marriage…fatherhood…divorce rushed towards him in the space of two and a half years—a time of anguish, guilt and regret, the only shining light his daughter. And then, a mere eight months after his divorce, Caroline had died behind the wheel of her Porsche, which she had been driving, he had been informed at the inquest, far too fast and with far too much booze in her system. She hadn't stood a chance when she had lost control in torrential rain.

So, yes, he had been immeasurably grateful to his aunt for being there. Right time, right place and a rock in stormy waters.

So this lady she had recommended? It would work.

His aunt was in her sixties and he presumed that her friend would be of similar age and thus not constrained by a daily commute to work or the trials and tribulations of a young family. Doubtless, the enormous pay cheque to cover the four weeks his aunt would be away would also ease matters somewhat.

With that in mind, he checked his watch and ordered another drink, barely glancing in the direction of the neatly uniformed waiter who sprinted towards him to take the order.

In this elegant five-star wine bar and with his daughter spending the night at the house of one of her friends, he would interview the Baxter woman, explain what would be expected of her and make sure she knew that the bulk of her pay cheque would be safely deposited into her bank account just as soon as her satisfactory interview with him was completed.

He was wholly assured that whoever his aunt recommended would be more than adequate. Evalina adored Annalise and would never suggest anyone she didn't have absolute faith in. But still…

When it came to hard cash, it paid to never take chances. His aunt's allotment pal might be as cosy as a patchwork quilt and as wholesome as apple pie, but he still intended to lay down the law and make sure the woman knew that, friendship or no friendship, he would be keeping a firm eye on her and slip-ups would not be tolerated. When it came to his daughter, normal rules of engagement definitely did not apply.

He glanced at his watch again and frowned.

She had approximately five minutes to make it to the wine bar and be positioned opposite him at the table he had reserved. Unreliability before day one had even begun was not going to impress.

He anticipated being back in time to cover a couple of hours of correspondence before he hit the sack at his usual post-work time of a little after midnight, and with another glance at his Rolex he settled in front of his phone and began scrolling through his emails.

Sophie Baxter made it to the wine bar with only seconds to spare and at speed.

Yet another protracted call to the bank, followed by one from the estate agent asking about party wall agreement documents, which had thrown her for six because she hadn't had much of a clue where to begin hunting those down…

She had already spent so long dealing with all the chaos and despair of life after her parents had died, and yet here she was now because suddenly, in the space of just a couple of days, life had gone flying off in a direction she could never have anticipated.

Lovely Evalina, her neighbour at the allotment she had managed to land seven months ago through a friend of a friend of a friend of a friend, had contacted her with a surprising offer that could not have arrived at a more fortuitous moment.

A month in a house nannying her nephew's six-year-old daughter, Annalise, whom Sophie had met only a fortnight or so ago and thoroughly liked.

'I know it's probably very last-minute, my dear, but the pay will be excellent...'

She had asked about an interview—surely she wouldn't be hired sight unseen? Her experience when it came to nannying, she had worriedly pointed out, was negligible. A few months with a family in France, where she had learnt a bit of French and had had a lovely time looking after their two young kids. It had been something of a gap year, but she had no formal qualifications...

But Evalina had vaguely waved away the suggestion. Speed was of the essence, she said, and her recommendation would carry sufficient weight with Niccolo—that and the fact that Sophie had met his daughter and they got along. There was no time for anything to be arranged, she had elaborated, because she had to leave the country immediately to help her sister and brother-in-law. There had been an accident—lots of broken bits and pieces, she had hinted darkly, without going into detail. Probably, Sophie concluded, because she found it too painful, something with which she could more than sympathise.

Sophie was guiltily aware that she had veered away from asking too many questions because the money had appealed, along with the fact that having somewhere to live for a month would tide her over until the stuff with the house had been sorted. It had felt like a reprieve and, after a year of horror and sadness and pain, a reprieve had been too good to pass up.

So now here she was, having an interview for a job she had already been offered, meeting an employer with only a description to go on: *'A very nice, very dutiful father, who works all hours to keep a roof over their heads. The poor, poor man lost his wife some years ago. That is why it is so important that he has faith in the person looking after his beloved daughter.'*

Tragic, Sophie had thought. Evalina's words had brought home to her all those memories of the accident that had taken both her parents in one fell swoop. A rainy night, a truck travelling too fast in the opposite direction…and suddenly lives ended far too soon. Sophie felt her life had ended there too, a little over a year ago, and so it had, in a way, because everything that had followed on could never be called *a life*. She had lurched her way through an unfolding horror story of pain as, bit by bit, her life unravelled in slow motion and the foundations underneath her that had always felt so secure crumbled away. She had had to deal with woes that she knew her parents had kept from her, financial problems that must have been slowly eating away at them for years. They had sheltered her from finding out the extent of their debts, all undertaken to put her through private school, all targeted to giving her the best possible head start in life. And then, with everything collapsing around her like a house of cards, she had made the biggest mistake of her life and sought comfort from the wrong guy.

Just thinking about it made her shudder.

So, whilst nerves had kicked in now as she paused in front of the chi-chi wine bar in Mayfair, it was a relief after months of numbing despair, with each day promising to deliver nothing new, just more of the same—debts to be paid, bills she hadn't known existed to be settled, and a future so unsteady that she couldn't bring herself to examine it in detail.

For the first time in months, she could feel a tiny ray of optimism trying to break through the dense storm clouds overhead and her nerves ratcheted up a couple of notches because she was *desperate* not to blow this opportunity.

She inhaled, exhaled, inhaled, exhaled, counted to ten and headed for the entrance of the wine bar.

Looking up from the report he had been reading, Niccolo saw the woman hovering in the doorway and drew in a sharp breath. She was arrestingly pretty yet he was surprised at how riveted he was by her blonde good looks because she was not at all the sort of woman he usually went for. He liked his women earthy, flamboyant, confident and on the same page as he was. Sexy, busty brunettes who didn't play coy games and never asked for more than he was willing to give.

His ex-wife, a refined Italian beauty with a pedigree as long as your arm, had charmed him with her softly spoken, coy, genteel cool. She had played hard to get, reaching out just so far before shyly pulling back. After four months and in a headlong rush of thwarted passion—partly driven, he had retrospectively concluded, by the fact that were he not so rich, she wouldn't have spared him a second glance—Niccolo had proposed.

Very quickly, he realised that with refinement came problems he just hadn't anticipated. The new Mrs Caroline Ferri of the impeccable lineage and the cut-glass accent—because she had been privately educated at a boarding school in the Shires—was agonisingly and, in the end, infuriatingly high maintenance. Her demands became imperious. She required constant attention and round-the-clock ad-ulation. She had Annalise but parenthood was not something she relished. As the only child of cold, distant parents who resided in regal splendour in Italy, she lacked any desire to bond with her child because her own parents had never bonded with her.

Niccolo, driven by ambition though he was, un-derstood the importance of family, and their lives veered off in different directions very quickly from that point.

The ending of their marriage had been in the making before it had really even begun, although he would always feel subliminal guilt about the way everything had unravelled—so quickly and so com-pletely.

He was adept at learning lessons. Promise nothing and look for less when it came to women. In the end, it was all about fun and sex. The obvious worked. The woman hovering nervously by the door was the opposite of obvious.

Tall and willowy, with her hair scraped back into some kind of bun, she was clutching her backpack in front of her with the tenacity of someone ward-ing off evil spirits.

But her face…perfectly heart-shaped with a small, straight nose and a full, inviting mouth. Her pink tongue flicked out, moistening her lips, and Niccolo was shocked at the sudden surge in his libido, which went from zero to ten in the space of seconds.

He fidgeted, returned to his phone and only raised his eyes again when he was aware of a shadow across the table.

In the space of time it took Sophie to approach the table where Niccolo was sprawled in a chair, staring at his mobile phone, she registered that this was not what she had been expecting.

By the time she was standing directly in front of him, her nerves had had time to multiply tenfold. She cleared her throat and shifted awkwardly. She felt like an idiot in this smart place. Her clothes were all wrong. Her capacious backpack was all wrong. She knew that she shouldn't be feeling like this. She had never been awed by expensive restaurants or flashy houses or idiotic, over-fast cars, but she felt awkward now, and she registered, subliminally, that it was the guy sitting in front of her who was encouraging that response.

Evalina had somehow managed to give the impression that her employer was a kindly, middle-aged, man—a devoted dad, a widower who had never quite got over the death of his wife. Details had been in scant supply, but Sophie had had no problem filling in all the gaps herself.

She had pictured a small, thin Italian gentleman who worked hard to make a good living. He would adjust his specs and they would have a comfortable conversation during which Sophie would do her utmost to reassure him that she would be a brilliant nanny for Annalise. She had done a lot of background research into things to do in London with young kids and all sorts of brochures were stuffed into her backpack, to be produced as evidence of her commitment.

This guy...

He looked as comfortable as a prowling shark in a tank full of minnows. He was younger than she had expected, mid-thirties perhaps, and his face was the perfect blend of beauty and power. Dark, dark eyes and raven-black hair cropped short so that nothing deflected from his harsh, stunningly perfect features. And where Evalina was slender and slight, her nephew was not. The opposite. He dwarfed the chair in which he was sitting.

In all respects, the man was breathtaking.

Apprehension threaded through her and her breathing quickened.

No, this was emphatically *not* what she had expected, and it certainly was not what she felt she could deal with at this moment in time. A too good-looking employer, free, single and unencumbered, who could get it into his head that his live-in nanny might be interested in some after-hours hanky-panky... Sophie wasn't vain, but she was realistic. She knew that her looks attracted attention just as much as she knew how much of a problem that could be. She'd learned how to ignore lascivious stares from men and protect herself, but she was still raw from her recent disastrous relationship and the last thing she knew she could emotionally handle would be a guy showing any kind of interest in her. At this moment in time, she just felt way too fragile to deal with anything like that.

She felt faint as she saw all of her hopes of some kind of breathing space fly through the window.

'Who are you?'

Sophie blinked. His voice matched his looks. Dark...exotic...strangely mesmerising.

'Sophie Baxter.' She held out her hand and wondered how she could phrase the beginning of her excuse for backing out of the arrangement his aunt had made. 'Your aunt? Evalina? She recommended me to you about the...er...vacancy for the nanny job to replace her now that she's had to return to Italy? I'm really sorry about your father, by the way. It must be worrying for you, stuck over here when you know he's been in an accident...'

'*You're* the woman my aunt has recommended?'

Sophie instantly felt her hackles rise. He sounded horrified.

'Sit.' He half rose, as though belatedly remembering that there was something called *common courtesy* and nodded to the chair opposite, and Sophie duly sat down, defences fully in place at his surprising reaction.

'Were you expecting someone else?' she asked politely, eyes reluctantly riveted to his dark face as he lounged back in the chair and looked at her with brooding intensity.

'You're younger than I expected,' Niccolo said flatly. 'When my aunt told me that one of her friends at the allotment would be perfect to stand in for her in her absence, I was expecting a woman of a similar age.'

'My apologies for being twenty-five,' Sophie replied coldly. 'I didn't realise there was an age threshold for the position. Evalina never mentioned that.'

Niccolo was working out that there was probably quite a bit his aunt had failed to mention, and not just to the blonde sitting in front of him with an expression that could freeze water—not that that had the slightest effect on him.

Up close, the woman was even more stunning than at a distance. Vanilla-coloured hair, eyes the most peculiar shade of blue, tall and slender. It seemed a catch-all description to describe her as a typical English rose, but this blue-eyed blonde had something he couldn't quite put his finger on, something that elevated her from the ranks of attractive blondes into something that had temporarily sent his libido into freefall.

Was it the unusual violet-blue of her eyes? Or the lushness of her lashes, dark in contrast to the white-blonde of her hair? Or the fullness of her mouth? Or maybe it was just because she was glaring at him, which wasn't the sort of reaction he was accustomed to getting from a woman.

At any rate, a twenty-five-year-old leggy blonde wasn't going to do and there was no point beating about the bush—although the prospect of putting work on hold indefinitely while he hunted down a suitable nanny didn't fill him with joy. He could, naturally, bring Annalise into his offices, arrange for his PA to keep an eye on her while he spent the day in back-to-back meetings, but how rewarding was that going to be for an energetic six-year-old who would want to be outside in the sunshine having some fun at the start of her summer holidays?

'Would you like something to eat?' He signalled to the waiter, who raced over, and he watched for a few seconds while she buried herself behind the oversized menu before emerging to shake her head.

'A cup of tea would be lovely.'

'A bottle of Chablis,' Niccolo drawled, 'and some tapas. Along with the cup of tea, of course.' He leant forward, hands on the table, and looked at her seriously for a few silent seconds. 'I apologise if you found my reaction rude,' he said.

'I get it. You thought that because I met your aunt at an allotment, I would be in my sixties, maybe without a partner and definitely without a nine-to-five job.'

Niccolo shrugged and laughed drily. He sat back, dark eyes roving over her face, appreciating the symmetry of her features and working out just why it was that his aunt had failed to provide him with an in-depth description of the woman she had recommended.

Evalina, like his parents, wanted to see him remarried. One tragic mistake, they were fond of telling him, was no excuse to remain a confirmed bachelor for the rest of his life. Annalise needed a mother and he needed the love of a good woman. Their exuberant Italian enthusiasm alternately amused and frustrated him. Respect compelled him to avoid confrontations on the issue but, thus far, they had backed off from the actual business of *matchmaking*.

He felt a surge of irritation that he had now been put in the awkward position of having to deal with a situation he hadn't envisaged.

'It had crossed my mind,' he admitted and then added, after a moment's hesitation, 'I think my aunt may have been playing games with both of us.' Why not be perfectly honest? When it came to addressing most thorny issues, honesty was usually the best policy as far as he was concerned. This was particularly true when it came to his dealings with the opposite sex. He liked things to be crystal clear, all cards on the table, for the avoidance of misunderstandings. He watched her closely, noted her frown as she thought about what he had just said and then also noted her flashbulb moment of comprehension.

'I see. At least I think I do.' Sophie sighed, amused despite herself by Evalina's manoeuvring. 'Your aunt thinks you…need to settle down? Is that it?'

Tapas and wine arrived, along with a pot of tea. Niccolo half smiled as she absently bypassed the tea and sipped some wine from the glass that had been poured. He shrugged.

'I am the only child of a traditional Italian family and that family very much includes my aunt, who sees me as something of a surrogate son, especially as my parents live in Italy. They are all of the opinion that marriage is what we everyone should aspire to.'

'Perhaps the fact that you have a young child also has something to do with it.' This man's personal life was none of her business, but she was relieved he had cleared the air because she didn't want complications and it would seem that neither did he.

He knew nothing about her aside from the fact that she came recommended by his aunt as someone who could be trusted with his daughter. She had brought her own references from the family she had nannied for in the past. That was the sum total of what he needed to know because her private life was hers and hers alone. If he wanted more formal qualifications, then he would have to look somewhere else. She would lose the lifeline she had been hoping for, but if the past year and a half had taught her anything it was that she could cope with whatever was thrown at her.

She knew nothing about him and had no intention of asking questions. Had he been happily married? Was he still in mourning for his late wife?

'Why me?' she heard herself ask, bluntly.

'Who knows? Maybe because you have a shared love of allotments.'

'I'm glad you've brought this out into the open. If I wasn't what you were expecting, then you weren't what I had expected either. If we're being honest, I can tell you that I looked at you and had already made up my mind that the job wasn't going to work out.'

'Sorry?'

He looked genuinely startled. Sophie grasped why. He was so good-looking, so crazily *sexy*, just so eminently *eligible* that he was probably accustomed to women seeking him out rather than shutting the door in his face.

Just for a moment—a very brief moment—Sophie enjoyed the thought of bringing him down a notch or two. Good-looking guys were always just a little too self-satisfied, and this one—far and away the most disconcertingly good-looking man she had ever met—would be more self-satisfied than most. Made sense.

'I…I'm recently out of a poor relationship with a guy I should never have gone near.' She didn't bother beating about the bush. 'I saw you and the last thing I felt I could deal with was the situation of sharing space with you and…'

Niccolo's face was moving swiftly from resignation at having to clear the air, to surprise that she hadn't reacted as expected, to downright stupefaction.

'You thought that I might turn out to be…*what*? Some kind of *sex pest*?'

'It's been known,' Sophie returned frankly.

'I can't believe I'm hearing this! I have *never*, repeat, *never* heard anything quite so outrageous in my life before!'

Sophie stood her ground and met his outraged midnight-dark eyes without flinching. She'd forgotten about the wine, and the plates of delicious tapas, and the pot of tea she had insisted on hadn't begun to register at all. She was consumed by his energy and immersed in a bubble where everyone and everything around her had morphed into white noise. She'd never felt the intensity of anyone's personality the way she was feeling this man's right now, and that alarmed and panicked her. And excited her. Although that was an emotion she stifled before it could take root and cause any damage.

Her heart was pounding.

'I should ask,' she said, breaking the electric silence but not the eye contact that held her spellbound, 'do you intend to employ me for the position or not? Because if not, then I'll make my way back home and won't waste either your time or mine any further.'

CHAPTER TWO

NICCOLO WAS BEGINNING to wonder how a straightforward path had managed to become so convoluted. Expectations of a homely, middle-aged spinster baking cakes with Annalise while he carried on with his hectic work life now seemed as ridiculous as believing in fairies at the bottom of the garden.

Should he have firmly but politely told the woman now looking stubbornly at him that the position was no longer on the table? No further explanations needed.

Rhetorical question because he knew the answer to that one: he should have. The minute he had clocked what his aunt was up to, he should have taken appropriate steps to ensure the situation was nipped in the bud.

He knew that neither Evalina, nor his parents, could fully understand just how bitter the lessons learnt during his marriage had been for him and all the more so because of the speed with which his life had raced out of control, veering over the side of the cliff before he had time to find a brake or a rudder or anything at all that could help control its devastating collapse. Nor would they ever understand how profoundly he had absorbed the ruinous path his parents had taken, content to work for nothing, to enjoy the simple pleasures of life without realising that simple pleasures were never enough. The day of reckoning would always come, and when it did, simple pleasures just didn't cut it. His father's day of reckoning, after years of working for a pittance in a company that had never been going to elevate him beyond a certain point, had come when he'd had a stroke. When he had had to retire from his job. What kind of future would they both have been facing had he, Niccolo, not had the wherewithal to rescue them? To give them the life he felt they deserved?

And his marriage? A fiasco. He had thought, against his better judgement, to find that elusive love and happiness his parents had been desperate for him to have. It had been a mistake, with his daughter the only good thing to emerge from the disaster. He could remember those endless times facing a ceaseless barrage of recrimination from his wife, the tug of war trying to balance work and play, with Caroline wanting *'fun and attention'* and viciously condemning when he failed to deliver. From the moment the ring had been put on her finger, life had changed for him.

Nothing was ever right, and living in a war zone had driven him to despair.

Silence had become his friend.

No one knew how deeply affected he had been, so, of course, any hint of compliance by hiring the woman should have been out of the question.

The last thing he needed was his aunt imagining that he had conceded to her Cupid tricks. That would be opening a Pandora's box.

On the other hand…

He was in a bind. He needed cover and he knew that there were some things you couldn't throw money at and get the required happy outcome.

The woman knew his daughter.

Was it any wonder he had hesitated? Why he had fought the impulse to do what his head had immediately told him to do? Why he had done the sensible thing and broached the thorny and delicate matter of laying down ground rules should he decide that he was prepared to go on his aunt's recommendations?

However much he disapproved of the reasoning behind said recommendations?

The fact that his first glimpse of her had taken his breath away had nothing to do with any subsequent decisions. The opposite! It had been all the more imperative to make it clear that he was out of bounds.

Whatever response he had anticipated, it hadn't been the one he'd received.

Who the heck was doing the interviewing here?

'Well?'

Still reeling from the shock of someone actually daring to think the unthinkable, Niccolo scowled.

'I've been put in an awkward position,' he returned, reasserting authority at speed. 'Evalina has vanished and I need help. So, to answer your question, the offer remains on the table with, as we have both acknowledged, certain conditions and ground rules in place.' He paused and searched for a less contentious footing from which to start their relationship. She was going to be in charge of his daughter, and a brooding and resentful nanny was the last thing he needed.

His eyes roved lazily over her cool, determined face and for the first time he found himself dealing with a situation he couldn't really remember having encountered before—an attractive woman who didn't automatically seek to please him.

He didn't want to stare or make her feel uncomfortable in any way, but hell, she was just so…spellbinding. The way she was dressed and the tightly pulled-back hair advertised someone wanting to downplay her assets, but nothing could quite extinguish her impact.

He looked away and shifted, annoyed with himself for being unable to control instincts he should be able to master.

'Tell me how you met my aunt,' he said abruptly, slamming shut the door on an imagination that was threatening to steer his responses. 'You seem, if you don't mind me saying, somewhat young to be working on an allotment.'

Sophie's heart was still pounding. He unsettled her in ways she couldn't quite understand. He had been open and honest with her, which had allowed her to be open with him in return. They had cleared the air. A little embarrassed, she wondered how she could have gone down the road of issuing warnings. The more she looked at him—and she couldn't seem to stop herself from looking—the more she realised that he was probably the last man on the planet to give the nanny a second glance.

The man oozed sinful sex appeal. He could snap his fingers and have any woman down tools and race towards him. Sophie knew that she was attractive enough, just as she knew that there were far more beautiful women out there than her and he was a guy who would have no problem getting any of them.

Had Scott, with his determined pursuit that had spanned so many years, somehow given her an inflated idea of how appealing she was to the opposite sex?

She had grown up with boys looking at her, but this wasn't a boy. This was a man, and he would certainly not be interested in a twenty-five-year-old woman with scant experience who was unsophisticated when it came to playing urbane, come-hither games with men.

She reddened just thinking about how misplaced her apprehensions had been, but then immediately reminded herself that it was better to be safe than sorry. She'd learnt that the hard way and it was a lesson she wasn't going to forget any time soon.

'I… They're very hard to come by in London.' Sophie felt as though she was releasing state secrets, even though she knew, realistically, that he was just asking the sort of normal questions any prospective employer would be asking. He wanted to find out about her, and that made sense given the role she would be accepting. Her nerves were all over the place, though. She could feel his dark eyes on her in a way that was disturbing and physical.

Was she making a mistake taking this job on?

She thought about the money problems that had plagued her since her parents had so suddenly and unexpectedly died and breathed in deeply. She had barely been able to mourn because her life had been thrown into such turmoil. She reminded herself how grateful she had been for Evalina's offer because the money would help clear some of the crushing debts.

Faced with that, what were a few harmless questions?

'I…I was actually studying land management at university…when…I had to cut short my course to deal with a few issues. I had a base in London, knew it well and decided to put my name down for an allotment, but before I could actually do that I found out a friend of a friend's grandfather was giving his up and I managed to secure it. I…I love gardening, had hoped to be a landscape gardener one day. Maybe that swung things in my favour. So many people don't look after their allotments the way they should.' She looked away and swallowed. She could feel her eyes welling up and wanted the ground to open and swallow her whole.

The thrust of a handkerchief against her clenched fist on the table was a shock.

'I think I must be one of the last people left in the world who still sees the value of a handkerchief.' He smiled. 'Take it. It's pristine, I promise.'

Their eyes tangled and Sophie nodded shakily.

'My apologies,' she said gruffly and was relieved when he moved swiftly along, acknowledging her apology with a shrug of his broad shoulders.

'You say you had *hoped* to be a landscape gardener one day?'

'Life had other plans,' Sophie said warily.

'And you would rather I didn't delve any further?'

'That's correct.' She held his gaze and refused to be sucked into over-confiding. What had Evalina told him about her? Not much, Sophie guessed, considering she had managed to leave out the most important fact, which was that she wasn't one of her contemporaries. In fairness, there wasn't much Sophie had told Evalina. Her grief still felt too raw, her heart-break too recent and her life in too much of a mess to detail, so she had kept the conversation light and bland and talked about plants and her love of them.

Sophie wondered whether Evalina would have started having mischievous notions if she had known how complicated her life really was, how very far from the straightforward plant-loving girl she really was.

She had spent ages with Annalise when she had visited the allotments, showing her the vegetable plants she had started to put in, the flowering plants that would bloom in time. It had been soothing. It had made her feel peaceful, had reminded her of the way her mother had patiently shared her own love of gardening.

The money was important and the fact that she would have a roof over her head for a while was also important, but Sophie felt that she had formed a bond with the little girl, which had played a great part in her accepting Evalina's offer.

Niccolo looked at her guarded expression and for the first time felt the kick of curiosity.

A man? A broken heart? A broken heart that had made her issue her crazy warning to him? What had happened to have caused her to quit a course that could have advanced her career?

He was surprised at how powerful the impulse

was to question her further about a personal life that was none of his business, because he had a marked lack of curiosity when it came to asking questions, possibly because he was so accustomed to women providing answers without much encouragement. The less you asked, the lighter things were, and he liked things light and breezy and uncomplicated.

'You have previously worked for a family as a nanny, I understand. My aunt mentioned something of the sort when she recommended you. I'm guessing this was before you embarked on your now abandoned university career?'

'I can provide references if you like.' She reached down to her backpack and pulled out a number of brochures. She casually rearranged the plates on the table, absently popping some kind of mini meat pastry into her mouth, making room for the paperwork.

Tendrils of hair were escaping the confines of all the clips she had used to tie it back.

Watching her, Niccolo distractedly thought that there was something fresh and genuine about her. Was that an illusion? He didn't go for the *butter wouldn't melt* types. He liked things straightforward and wasn't interested in the usual courting games that presumed a conclusion involving a bridal shop and a walk up an aisle.

He also didn't do cut-glass accents and boarding-school backgrounds. Having entered that world with his ex, he now stayed true to his own background.

Definitely smoky singer in a club as opposed to soprano diva at an opera.

On all fronts, Sophie Baxter didn't make the grade, so why was he so compelled to look? What was it about her that stirred his imagination?

Whatever it was, it wasn't going to do, and it annoyed him that for once he was finding it difficult to rein in his responses.

She raised her eyes, true blue that almost veered into violet, and he shifted uncomfortably in the chair once again.

When she thrust a piece of paper towards him, he reluctantly took it and read a glowing recommendation from the family for whom she had nannied three years previously.

Oddly, and if he'd wanted any further reassurances about taking her on, he knew the family in question. He had done business with the guy only a handful of months previously. He was as solid, as respectable and as trustworthy as they came. Small world, but he knew only too well that it was a village when it came to people who were filthy rich.

'How did you find this family?'

Sophie hesitated. She thought of her darling parents, struggling without her knowing to maintain a façade, and all for her. To keep her at the expensive private school, to fund the university fees and the holidays and a lifestyle she could happily have done without.

Two people who had started out comfortably enough, she guessed, from weeks of scouring a million bank statements and a thousand receipts. Her father had been a partner at an accountancy firm and her mother had been a very happy housewife.

At some point within the past five years, things had gone horribly wrong. A poor investment had spread all sorts of toxic tentacles through their finances and, reading between the lines, Sophie had sensed the panic that must have overwhelmed her dad because he had thrown bad money after good in an attempt to staunch the haemorrhaging of cash. With a mortgage still on their house in London and bills to pay, she could only imagine how fearful he must have been.

The heady days when he had known the likes of Eric and Lina Buhler seemed like a lifetime ago now that she was sitting here, remembering those times of innocence.

She wasn't going to go down any roads of sharing confidences, though. Niccolo had made it very clear that lines of demarcation between them had to be in place for this to work.

However much she found him disconcerting, she wasn't going to nervously impart any information that wasn't strictly necessary, and it wasn't necessary for him to know anything about her parents. He was free to assume what he wanted.

'They were recommended to me.' She lowered

her eyes. 'I enjoy skiing and I wanted a bit of time out before uni. It seemed like a good idea and it was great fun. I loved it and I got along very well with the Buhlers. They are a lovely family. I haven't done any nannying since then, but I've met your daughter and we've clicked.' She nudged the brochures and pamphlets towards him and Niccolo duly scooped the top two up and perused them.

Museums…a Disney art exhibition…the zoo…lots of gardens… She'd done her due diligence and that impressed him because she obviously hadn't taken anything for granted simply because she came with his aunt's blessing. She was leaning towards him, her white-blonde hair escaping around her flushed cheeks, her violet eyes one hundred per cent focused on him, her lips slightly parted.

'Good.' He sat back and looked at her carefully. 'And will there be any impediment to your living with Annalise and me for the duration of your tenure? This is important to me because as much as I try, it's impossible to dictate my working hours. You'll need to be on hand to cover those times when I can't make it home…as early as I would like.' He paused, guiltily aware that far too often he worked late, and with his aunt there he had become too comfortable with long hours. In the wake of his failed marriage and after his wife had died, Niccolo had striven to work normal hours, but it was difficult running his sprawling empire between the strict hours of nine to five. He had all the money in the world but not enough time. Work was his fortress and it had been easy to sit behind those impregnable walls, controlling the direction of his life, but had he somehow become a less than effective father in the process? He adored his daughter, but was adoration enough? Things, he suspected, would have to change with a new woman on the scene. He would have to be physically present to keep an eye on proceedings.

'What sort of impediment?'

'Parents? A relative you may be looking after? Unresolved boyfriend issues? Cats? Dogs? Goldfish?'

'I…' She paused as she blindly sought the handkerchief she had rested on her lap. 'No, there won't be any impediment.'

Niccolo looked at her for a few moments, head tilted to one side, then he sat forward and briskly slapped both hands on the table. 'Right. Here's what is going to happen next. You'll get a contract from my PA, which you will be required to sign.' He named a weekly salary that he could hear took her breath away. 'That will be your basic pay,' he said. 'Purely covers nine to five. You start work earlier or end later and you will be compensated accordingly.' He paused. 'I hope you don't think that we got off on the wrong foot, Miss Baxter—'

'Sophie, please.' She tried a smile on for size.

'And of course, you must call me Niccolo.'

'And no, I don't think we got off on the wrong foot. Makes it easier, knowing that…'

'That there will be no unpleasant mixed messages? Agreed. Moving on… I will expect you on Monday at eight a.m. sharp. I have a series of meetings but I can push them back so I can show you the ropes.' He hesitated. 'I may work long hours, but let there be no mistake: my daughter is the centre of my life, and I am putting a great deal of faith in you that you won't let me down.'

'I won't.'

'Whether I am physically in the house or not, there will be a strict rule in place that there are no parties…or men sleeping over…'

'There won't be!'

'You'll be relinquishing your free movement for a few weeks,' he elaborated gently. 'Whatever situation you may have been through that's brought you here…' He found himself pausing, giving her time to jump in. She didn't. 'You're young and you might find it difficult having your wings temporarily cut to some degree, and I say to some degree because you will naturally have your time to do as you wish outside the house whenever I am at home. I intend to spend as much of the weekends as possible working from home.'

'Can I ask you something?'

'I'm all ears.' He made a magnanimous, sweeping gesture with one hand and relaxed back.

'Do you *ever* stop working?'

For the second time that evening, Niccolo was knocked for six.

His aunt nagged him about the hours he worked. So did his parents. He indulged them.

Beyond those privileged three, no one had ever broached the subject, including the many women he had dated in the past. He'd never had to make a point of it. Perhaps they had all read invisible warnings he had projected and steered clear from a topic that would spell the end of any relationship.

He had emerged from a broken marriage where the hours he worked had become a bone of contention, always to be used whenever an attack was to be made.

He had no intention of returning to that place. Reproving dark eyes clashed with calm, serene violet ones.

'How I choose to spend my time is of no concern to you and has no bearing on this job,' he said coolly, and he was perversely even more furious when she shrugged.

'Of course, I understand,' Sophie murmured, dropping her eyes.

'What exactly is it that you understand?'

'I'll be paid to do a job and part of that job is

never to ask any questions. You give orders and I obey them.'

'That's not quite the situation as I see it,' Niccolo inserted. 'Whatever questions you ask about your duties will be welcomed. Beyond that, everything is off limits.'

'Of course.'

'I'll expect regular briefings, but my plan, as I said, is to try and limit my working hours while my aunt is away.' He felt restless, edgy. It wasn't just that the woman wasn't what he had been expecting. There was something about her that unsettled him, that derailed his usual cool, clear thought processes and encouraged wayward thoughts.

'If I choose not to go out…er…when you're around, would I be expected to…? I'm assuming that it would be okay for me to retire to my bedroom?'

'Of course. This is a business arrangement, Sophie. I don't expect you to hover in the background waiting for instructions when I'm in the house. I'll take over the minute I return home and you're then free to do whatever you want.'

He couldn't have given a more clear-cut answer and yet there was something that didn't feel quite as businesslike an arrangement as it should, and she wondered whether that was because she was so *aware* of him. He made every nerve in her body go into full alert mode, made the hairs on the back of her neck stand on end. In every way he was compelling, and she wondered how this arrangement, which had seemed such a godsend at the time, was actually going to work.

She couldn't possibly vacate the house every evening. She couldn't afford to go anywhere, for a start. She'd also, in the aftermath of her unravelling life, discovered just how unreliable good friends could be. When they'd thought she had money, when she'd been one of them, they'd been there, happy to socialise, keen to drag her out to whichever club was the flavour of the month, even if she would rather have stayed in. And when everything had come crashing down and life as she'd known it had become a thing of the past, they had sympathised, but honestly, where were they now?

Invites had dried up and she would have struggled to find the cash to go anyway. When you mixed with the rich crowd, they quickly lost patience, she had found, with anyone who couldn't keep up, and there was no way she could any more.

Only a handful of friends had stuck by her, for which she was grateful, but she knew that they tactfully avoided asking her to places that cost a lot, and there were only so many occasions when they wanted to entertain at home.

She had vacated one world and entered another and this new world did not accommodate lots of after-work activities. Even going solo to the movies would require thought because every penny saved was a penny towards paying off the bills that needed sorting.

So she would be confined to her bedroom, hesitant about venturing out when he was there because she didn't want to bump into him, though it was likely inevitable. How big was his house going to be, after all?

When she thought about that, her head felt woozy at the series of uncomfortable images suddenly crowding in, jostling for space.

She pictured him relaxed, in a pair of jeans and a T-shirt, barefoot and roaming at all hours of the day and night, turning her every waking moment into a cat-and-mouse game just to avoid the peculiar effect he had on her nervous system.

'There'll be no need for you to do anything of a household nature,' he belatedly added. 'I have someone who comes in daily for a couple of hours to clean and a dedicated chef on standby. Of course, my aunt would have nothing to do with anyone getting under her feet in the kitchen...'

Sophie smiled and relaxed when she thought about Evalina. 'I know. I don't think she appreciates anyone touching her homegrown produce on the allotment either. She's very competitive when it comes to what everyone else grows. My beans never seemed to be quite as good as hers, as she very kindly pointed out on one occasion. Not as long and definitely not as fat and juicy. She offered to bring a measuring tape to prove it.'

Niccolo burst out laughing. 'Evalina is never backward when it comes to speaking her mind.'

'Has she always been like that?'

'As far back as I can recall. Two sisters and they couldn't have been more different. My mother was the dutiful wife and Evalina was the nomad who travelled the world.'

'Yes, she's told me a lot about her adventures.' Curiosity crept stealthily through her, making a mockery of her vow to remain uninterested and detached. Ground rules, after all, had been laid down on both sides but the temptation to side-step them was too great. There was something about the depth of his eyes, the tug of the forbidden pulling her to go beyond the lines he had laid down. 'I'm an only child so I wouldn't know, but isn't it odd that sisters can be so different? How lovely that your mum was there for you while Evalina travelled. She must have wafted in and brought lots of excitement when she came.'

Niccolo hesitated. 'She did,' he admitted. 'My parents led a very...predictable life. Evalina brought the scent of adventure. To a young child like me, it was always a thrill having her around.'

'Annalise adores her.'

'She does.'

* * *

He wondered how they had made it to this topic. Her eyes were calm and interested but nothing about her manner suggested anything other than the sort of polite small talk that might happen at the tail end of a conversation.

He hadn't shut the conversation down, as he normally would have, because she wasn't trying to wheedle her way into his affections. She'd be living under his roof, he uneasily decided, so where was the harm in a bit of harmless chit-chat? They could hardly plan on spending the next few weeks in a state of freezing silence, interrupted only by exchanges about Annalise.

Even so…

This would not become a trend. He wasn't going to be settling down to cosy evenings in, chatting about this, that and nothing in particular, simply because she happened to be temporarily living with him.

He wasn't going to forget that she was there for a very specific reason.

He abruptly relegated that brief lapse to the history books. 'Naturally, you'll want to return to your home to see your parents in your free time. In which case, you can bring as much or as little as you think you'll need when you move in on Monday…'

Sophie reddened. For a few seconds, she appeared

lost for words, struggling to find some kind of co-
herent response.

'I…no, I don't live with my parents.' She glanced
away, as though waiting for him to pick up the thread
of the conversation and move on to something else,
but he didn't. His eyes bored with laser intensity into
her as he waited for her to speak.

'I… Actually, my family home is in the process
of being sold…so…'

'When?'

'When what?'

'When are you due to move out?'

'I… The new occupants will be moving in in a
few weeks' time.' She rubbed her temples and appeared startled when he reached across the table and
brushed her wrist with his finger.

'Are you all right, Sophie?'

'Of course!' She smiled brightly.

'If you've always lived in the family home then
it would be upsetting to think of moving house.' He
looked at her, expression shuttered, noting the way
she couldn't meet his eyes. The smile was bright.
The eyes were telling a different story.

'These things happen,' she said stiffly.

She finally looked at him and her violet eyes were
defiant. Niccolo appreciated her stubborn refusal to
pour her heart out. There was a story there, but she
had no intention of telling it. She had her boundar-

ies and, for a man who had his, that was something to be respected.

'They do,' he murmured smoothly and called for the bill. 'My driver can collect you on Monday along with whatever possessions you want to bring with you for the duration of your contract.'

'No! It's fine. I can always return if I need more stuff,' she expanded, evading his searching gaze.

'In that case…' Bill paid, Niccolo began rising to his feet and Sophie hurriedly followed suit, reaching down for her backpack and scooping up all the pamphlets and brochures still on the table. 'Like I said, my PA will be in touch with all the details, and I look forward to seeing you next week.' He held out his hand to shake hers and a jolt of electric charge shot through him, as powerful as though he'd suddenly been plugged into a live socket.

CHAPTER THREE

Sophie realised several things very quickly the following Monday when she showed up for duty promptly at eight a.m. wheeling her suitcase behind her and burdened by an assortment of various other bags.

The first was that she wouldn't be popping back to the family home on a regular basis. Of course, she would return once every few days to check the post, but, since nearly all the companies she was dealing with now had her email address, physical bills through the door were scant. The truth was, the second she shut that front door behind her, turning around for one last look at the pretty Georgian edifice that had been the bedrock of her entire life, she had felt a sense of release.

With military efficiency, the contract Niccolo had mentioned had been in her message box within two hours of her leaving the wine bar, and the stipulated duration of her employment would be a month, on an eye-wateringly generous pay package.

A month away from being in the family home, with its sad reminders of better times and memories of how much love she had known within those walls, had seemed like manna from heaven.

Any uncertainties she had entertained over the weekend about Niccolo and his peculiar, unwelcome effect on her had dissipated, and by the time she had lugged her case to the front door of his London mansion she had convinced herself that this month away would mark a turning point in her life.

On that optimistic note, she had been dismayed to find that her glib assumption that he couldn't possibly be as disturbing as she had originally thought was way off target.

When he had answered the door the breath left her body in a whoosh and she momentarily lost all power of speech.

He was taller than she'd recalled, sexier than she'd remembered, and as much of a challenge as she'd sincerely hoped he wouldn't be.

But she'd swallowed back her unwelcome response, allowed him to carry her cases and various bags in, somehow managing to reply when he'd asked her, with amusement, whether she hadn't found the journey on public transport a little tedious with so much stuff.

He had been scrupulously polite as he'd shown

her to her room, a word which did no justice to the sweeping suite which would be her home from home for the next few weeks.

Thank goodness for Annalise, who had hopped along with them, an unwitting chaperone keeping nerves at bay and allowing her to have something else to focus on—though not even that little hand slipped into hers could distract from Niccolo's overwhelming presence.

It had been a relief when he had finally excused himself to leave for the office.

Annalise, a beautiful child with long dark hair, was a joy. Having only seen her at the allotment when she had been there with Evalina, Sophie now relished the chance to get to know her better.

She had numerous activities lined up, but in the end it was a bright day, warm and cloud-free, and so they took a picnic to the allotment and spent much of the day there, peacefully weeding and planting and going through some of the gardening books Sophie stored in her little shed.

They brought out two deckchairs at lunchtime and chatted, and she was glad for the easy tranquillity, which soothed her troubled mind.

Annalise reminded Sophie of herself as a child: quiet, thoughtful, curious.

How had her mother's death, she wondered, affected the little girl? She would have been young at the time, but of course Evalina would have been there for her. And her father.

The minute Sophie began thinking about Niccolo, her mind went off at a tangent and it was next to impossible to rein it in.

And yet…for all that…for the first time in a very long time, she felt *alive*, capable of thoughts that weren't depressing and inward turned.

Even when she had been fool enough to be persuaded into a relationship with Scott, she hadn't felt so…alert, so stimulated…so aware that there was life happening out there still…

It puzzled her how one perfect stranger should have kickstarted such a fundamental change in her, but perhaps she'd lived for so many months dealing with everything on her own that just coming into contact with someone else, someone disassociated with what she was going through, accounted for her reaction.

That and the fact that the man is impossibly good-looking, a little voice whispered inside her head.

Disillusioned though she'd been after Scott, and determined as she had been to give men a wide berth for the foreseeable future, she was still, it would seem—against all odds—a woman capable of feeling things even if those things happened to be things she didn't want to feel.

Having convinced herself that the mansion he lived in was plenty big enough for them to co-exist without too much crossover—and besides, he would be hard at work until who knew what time of the night—she was taken aback when, after a day at the allotment and part of the afternoon at the park near by, she opened the door to find that her employer was not conveniently holed up wherever he worked. He greeted them, larger than life, emerging from one of the doors that led out of the spectacular highly polished marble hallway, where two small Picasso paintings sat alongside a more substantial Hockney.

'You're here.' Sophie walked slowly towards him while Annalise flew ahead before screeching to a stop as though suddenly aware that she shouldn't fling herself into her dad's arms but perhaps shake his hand instead.

From what Sophie had seen, there was certainly love and affection in abundance there, but it didn't seem to transmit into hugs and kisses.

Had those hugs and kisses been the domain of his wife—Annalise's mother?

Their eyes met over Annalise's dark head and Sophie blushed.

'I thought I'd return early as you're still finding your feet and we haven't had a chance to chat about the arrangements.' He ruffled his daughter's hair and smiled down at her before once again looking at Sophie, moving slowly towards her while Annalise fell into step alongside him.

'Good!' Sophie said brightly. She wondered

whether he was checking up on her and thought that that was to be expected and a good thing, in a way.

'It's after five-thirty.' Still in his work clothes, he glanced at his Rolex then back to her. 'Why don't you go and freshen up? I will sort out my daughter's dinner and have some time with her, then I'll order some dinner for us and you can debrief me on how your day today has been, fill me in on anything you feel I should know.'

Sophie hovered. Dinner together? When she'd thought about their infrequent meetings to discuss Annalise, she'd imagined something more formal. Not requiring a suit, a briefcase and a PowerPoint presentation, but not a million miles off.

She opened her mouth to tell him that she would be more than happy to settle Annalise but then, looking at the rapt expression on the little girl's face, she realised that her father taking time out to spend with her was not an everyday occurrence. It was something to get excited about.

'You look like a rabbit caught in the headlights,' he murmured, standing directly in front of her now, and looking down into her upturned face. 'No need to panic. It won't be the Spanish Inquisition.'

'Of course not,' Sophie returned in the same bright voice, her expression glazed. 'But my feet haven't had a chance to really touch the ground, and of course I'm nervous at the thought that you might want to quiz me because you don't trust me.'

She started when he leaned close to her, close enough for her to feel his warm breath when he whispered, lazily, 'I trust you, Sophie. If I didn't, I would have had you followed. You come recommended by my aunt, though, and to do such a thing would have gone against the grain. So relax. We're going to be in one another's company for the next few weeks. You're going to have to learn not to look at me as though I might bite.'

He drew back but his dark eyes were still pinned to her face and he was smiling, eyebrows raised, his expression amused but watchful.

Was he playing games with her? No, he was being utterly serious. He really *would* have had her followed, and the thought of that sent a shiver down her spine.

He might be the perfect gentleman and together they might have worked out their boundary lines, but he was leaving her in no doubt that he called the shots.

She was pretty sure he would have checked up on her references. Had he also checked up on *her*? Unearthed her past? How much of her life was still private?

The questions pinged in her head for the next hour and a half as she roamed around her suite of rooms, too anxious to appreciate her luxurious surroundings.

Her massive bedroom overlooked an actual *gar-*

den big enough for flowerbeds and a paved area with extensive seating. There was also a massive en suite bathroom and a sitting area with a television. It wasn't Evalina's—not unless he had had the wardrobes cleared of all her clothing—which meant that she would have her own quarters somewhere else. It was a four-storeyed house. It made her parents' place, which she had always considered big, look like a doll's house in comparison.

She'd spent most of her formative years mixing with the wealthy. Here she had a glimpse of how those people several hundred steps above actually lived.

She'd brought what she'd considered suitable and sufficient, provided she kept on top of the laundry. After a long bath, which felt like the very height of luxury because this place was like a hotel, and if she closed her eyes she could forget that her nagging problems were just a heartbeat away, she changed into jeans, a T-shirt and some espadrilles and headed down to the kitchen.

She'd barely had time since she'd arrived to explore the house because it had felt rude, but without Annalise next to her she opened a few doors and looked into a series of spectacular rooms.

In the hallways pale wood replaced the marble used in the wide entrance hall, and the rugs were silk and looked priceless, co-ordinating with the art on the walls, which also looked priceless. It was an uncluttered modern house that just escaped being minimalist.

She hesitated outside the kitchen door, which was ajar, and then pushed it open on a deep, steadying breath.

Niccolo looked up from where he was sitting at the kitchen table, laptop open in front of him, and half rose, nodding to the seat opposite him. She duly slid into it and rested her hands on the table.

'Glass of wine?' he offered, reaching for the bottle of red in front of him, and Sophie shook her head. 'Tell me about your day.'

'Hasn't Annalise told you what we did?'

'I'd like to hear your version.'

She smiled stiffly and relayed how they had spent the day, from beginning to end. She fidgeted under his steady, dark gaze, shying away and back to feeling as though she was in the witness box, being asked deceptively easy questions that might or might not be leading straight into quicksand. He had a watchful way about him that made her want to babble. It also made her want to defend herself, even though she didn't know what she should be defending herself against because he hadn't accused her of anything.

Eventually her voice tapered off, at which point he said, matter-of-factly, 'I didn't have you followed but I did do a few rudimentary checks on you…'

Sophie didn't say anything. Of course he had. It would have been an oversight of his not to have done so. Trusting his aunt was one thing but no one got to the top of the food chain by being a fool.

Still, she felt violated.

How much did he know about her? She'd always been a private person and events over the past year and a half had made her even more so. She had dealt with all the money issues, with all the emotional issues, on her own, and thinking that this sloe-eyed sexy stranger *knew* some of her history sent a ripple of alarm and panic racing through her.

Logic and reason had no part in her sudden tension and the overpowering temptation to tell him that her life was none of his business.

'Your parents…' Niccolo said quietly.

She wasn't looking at him.

'Why didn't you do your background checks before I came to the interview?' She looked at him with bitter, accusing eyes.

'I wanted to meet you first. I imagine you've had a tough time of things and I'm very sorry about your parents, Sophie.'

'It's none of your business.'

'Your background became my business when I agreed to hire you to look after my daughter.'

Sophie sighed and looked at him. 'They died in a car accident,' she said quietly. 'It was rainy. My dad lost control. They hadn't been drinking and it wasn't even really all that late at night either. It was just one of those things.' She hadn't spoken about this to anyone in a long time. She had held it all to herself while life carried on around her, amidst the sadness and the confusion. She'd thought it would be difficult to actually talk about what had happened, but now that she had begun, she could feel a sense of release sweeping over her.

'I was at uni. I had a career ahead of me and then just like that life came crashing down and I was drowning.'

She realised that this was now the second time in a matter of days that a man who was, really, a complete stranger had brought her close to crying. She wished she'd hung on to that handkerchief. There was a river of tears inside her and she knew that it was going to burst its banks and overflow, but suddenly she didn't care.

'I was very close to my parents. They were ripped away from me and I just couldn't really cope.' She held her head in her hands and stared down at the smooth surface of the table, not bothering to try and staunch the tears that had been a long time coming. She felt them leak out and then there he was. How had he moved so quickly to put his arms around her?

Suddenly, that physical contact seemed the most comforting thing in the world.

She was dampening his shirt. She also wanted to blow her nose. After a few seconds, she drew in a shuddering breath and sat back and said, prosaically, 'I'm sorry. Your shirt's wet.'

'It'll live to fight another day. I have another hand-kerchief.'

'A constant supply.'

'Like I said, old habits die hard. My father was a fan of handkerchiefs. Inherited trait. Tell me what happened, Sophie.'

She wanted to. It was the strangest thing. Had she bottled everything up for so long that all it took was a kind word from a stranger for the dam to burst?

She talked about her parents, remembering small details and smiling at the memories. She could sense some of the darkness leaving her. It felt good to let it all out of her system.

'You probably know that I have considerable money problems,' Sophie said in conclusion as she finally looked at him, in control of herself now. 'I suppose that would have been one of the first things any background check would have thrown up.' She sighed. 'It all came out in the wash. Poor invest-ments, over-extension on the mortgage… They did everything within their power to keep me in the life I was accustomed to.' She pressed fingers over her eyes and rubbed them wearily. 'They didn't think to ask me whether any of that mattered or not.'

'And would it have?'

'No!' She laughed bitterly. 'Private school was fine. The classes were small and the surroundings were amazing, but the other kids… Some were great, but a lot were privileged and entitled and downright annoying.'

Niccolo smiled.

'I've met a fair few of the entitled and privileged in my time,' he admitted drily, 'and I must say I agree wholeheartedly with your sentiments.'

'I took this job for a lot of reasons,' Sophie told him truthfully. 'Of course, I really do like kids, and I really do like your daughter. She's…very special.'

'But you also need the money.'

'I'm not materialistic,' Sophie automatically protested, and he raised his eyebrows wryly.

'Have I levelled that accusation at you?'

Sophie shrugged. 'I've had to sell an awful lot of things to pay off all the debts that just kept coming on a daily basis.' She grimaced. 'I also had to sell the family home. It still had a mortgage but there should be sufficient money made from the sale to clear the majority of the debt. So yes, I took the job because I need the money. And being here for a month? It buys me a bit of breathing space while I decide what happens next now the house is sold and there's nothing left but memories to pack up.'

'Would you return to your studies?'

Sophie laughed without humour. 'I don't think that's on the cards. It's a luxury I can't run to. Maybe one day. No, for now I'm compiling a résumé to go into landscape gardening. It's something I would love to do and it's possible someone out there might be prepared to give me a chance.' She paused and looked at him without flinching. 'Working on the allotment will help. I've got an excellent idea of how harmonious spaces can be created with vegetables and fruits and plants built around office spaces so that people can work and simultaneously be calm and relaxed. I think I could put together some good ideas on how this concept could be turned into something really special.'

Another first. Talking about a plan for the future. She scooped up her hair with one hand and then absently began braiding it into one thick plait while she looked at him uncertainly.

'I suppose you're going to tell me that my services are no longer required...'

'Come again?'

'I realise I...must have come across as...as... something of an emotional train wreck and I can only think that that's a trait you might not want in an employee.'

'You lost your parents without warning and you've been dealing with the wreckage of what was left behind,' Niccolo said gently. 'So, do I consider you an emotional train wreck? No. I don't.' He looked at her steadily. 'In fact,' he continued pensively, 'it helps that you need the money. I sense you'll be prepared to go the extra mile when it comes to working more hours, and as an added incentive I will escalate your pay on a sliding scale. The later you work and the more demands I find I need to make of you, the more your pay will rise.'

'There's no need to do that. You're already paying me far more than I could get anywhere else.'

'I will also send someone to help you collate the things you want to keep from your family home and I'll arrange the necessary storage.'

'I don't feel comfortable with that.'

'Why not?'

'Because…it's not part of the job. If I were to get a regular nanny job through a regular nanny agency, there's no employer who would do favours like that.'

'I can afford it and let's call it buying your loyalty and ensuring my trust in you isn't misplaced. I will arrange for half of the money to be transferred to your account tomorrow with the other half to follow when your stint is at an end. While you're here, you're to put everything pertaining to Annalise on expenses and I'll ensure you have a separate credit card for that purpose and a few hundred quid in petty cash.'

Sophie gasped, with a shade of discomfort. 'A few hundred pounds in petty cash? That's very generous.'

'Yet you look as though you're tempted to turn down the offer. I wouldn't get into a lather about it, Sophie. Anyone casting an eye over the accounts that cover the payroll for my many, many companies will find one thing in common: I pay well. Over the odds. Substantially so. I find that the fatter the pay

cheque the more loyal the employee, and for me, loyalty is everything.'

'You like buying people,' Sophie mused, then reddened because the remark was inappropriate, given
that he was her boss. He appeared to think about
what she'd said, though, and when he spoke, softly,
it was to concur.

'I find it works,' he murmured.

On a subconscious level, Niccolo acknowledged that
that had been ingrained into the fabric of his life for
a very long time. He had seen how his parents had
lived their lives—dependent and in the service of
those higher up the pecking order—and it was a life
he had chosen to reject.

For Niccolo, that rejection meant rising and rising
fast to a place where he was dependent on no one,
a place where no one could ever call the shots and
expect him to follow. He would never be a follower.
The collapse of his marriage had taught him that
the path he had chosen was just not compatible with
the demands of any relationship that required exhaustive emotional input. Everything had imploded
quickly with Caroline, all done and dusted in under
four years, but had it stretched out for longer, would
it have been any more successful? No.

Yet no one had ever pointed that out to him quite
so bluntly. He was disconcerted to find himself suddenly and thankfully very briefly questioning that

firmly held belief, the lodestar which had guided his life.

'Food.' He cut short the conversation and stood up. 'I can order something in.'

'I…' Was this going to be a habit? Sophie wondered. She was acutely conscious of the very personal information she had shared, even though the information had already been in his domain. She had embellished the bare bones, had released so many feelings, and something was telling her now that that kind of release was utterly inappropriate, given their situation.

It wasn't simply the fact that she was being paid by him to do a job. It was because he was a man who put money and what it could buy, including people, over and above everything else.

He might be a good listener, but it would be a mistake to be lulled into thinking that she could vent to him about what she had gone through. She couldn't. In fact, when she thought about that, about another intimate conversation, she felt a shiver of apprehension.

'You've been here a handful of minutes,' Niccolo said briskly. 'I don't expect you to scuttle up to your bedroom, hungry and disoriented because I don't want company. You needn't fear that you'll be compelled to dine with me whenever I'm here. In fact, my hours are so unpredictable that that would be impossible anyway.'

'Good.' Sophie smiled.

'Interesting response,' Niccolo said wryly. 'Are you usually this forthright? No, scratch that. I think I've already reached the conclusion that you are. Dinner? What do you want?'

'I don't mind. Thank you.'

'In which case,' Niccolo drawled, 'I'll see what's available here and wing it.'

He spun round and walked towards the fridge and peered inside.

Sophie wanted to drag her eyes away from him but she couldn't. The way he moved, fluid and economic, was arresting. She could almost *see* the flex of powerful muscles under the T-shirt and the faded jeans.

How on earth could she have actually poured her heart and soul out to him? The ease with which she had opened up baffled and scared her because she had been so determined never to trust a man again. At least not until she was strong enough to deal with it.

'You…er…cook?' she asked politely, breaking the silence and watching as he took stuff out of the fridge.

As with the rest of the impressive house, everything in the kitchen seemed to be beyond expensive, from the metal and granite table where she was seated, to the pale, oversized tiles on the floor and the dull brushed chrome of the appliances. It was a marvel of grey and white that was both functional and aesthetically beautiful at the same time.

Niccolo turned to look at her for a few seconds.

It was a relief to have put some physical distance between them.

Back to business. He had laid his cards on the table, told her what his background checks had uncovered, and she had been open with him. No, he hadn't expected the conversation to be quite so emotional, although he should have predicted it, but he had risen to the occasion and she had quickly regained her self-control.

She clearly had no interest in shared meals and that suited him fine, even if it *was* a first for him.

She could be a distraction. Something about her got under his skin and he was very happy to take whatever steps were necessary to avoid dealing with that unexpected occurrence.

He would want to communicate with her often about Annalise, but he could easily do so in the relative formality of his home office.

Looking at her now, he caught himself thinking, once again, how very unusual her eyes were, then he snapped out of it and said with a self-deprecating shrug, 'I'm Italian. I grew up with my father at the stove. I used to stand on a chair, watching him make pasta.'

'That sounds wonderful.'

'I don't have time to do very much cooking these days.' Niccolo wasn't looking at her. He was chopping tomatoes, smelling the herbs he had extracted from the fridge and thinking how long it had been since he had lifted a hand in the kitchen. And when it came to women...

Home-cooked meals at the kitchen table definitely weren't on the agenda.

He was always upfront about his lack of interest in anything remotely permanent, but just in case the message wasn't relayed in sufficiently loud and clear tones he made it a priority to give no encouragement.

His home was his space where he spent time with his family. He had a penthouse apartment in Mayfair, and that was where he spent time with whatever woman he happened to be seeing.

Hot nights and no sleepovers.

'That's a shame. I expect cooking for other people is a bit like gardening is for me. Something restful that takes the stress out of everyday life.'

'I find a chef can do that just as well.'

He expertly threw ingredients into a frying pan, smelling and seasoning as he went, flicking the pan with his hand so that the chopped vegetables somersaulted in the olive oil and butter.

'It'll be ten minutes.' Niccolo turned to her and for a few seconds their eyes tangled, and he drew in a sharp, unsteady breath.

She'd admitted to a lot, he realised, probably a lot

more than either of them had expected. He had inadvertently opened a door to an outpouring of emotion
that had been bottled up for months while she dealt
with the material fallout from her parents' death.

So much revealed and yet...on one matter she had
been conspicuously silent.

*What about the guy who'd made her bitter enough
to be cautious when she had first met him? Where
did he figure in this whole scheme of things?*

And suddenly there it was again...curiosity. The
last thing he needed...

CHAPTER FOUR

'SHALL WE COUNT the number of floors?'

But that was never going to be possible. Neither she nor Annalise stood any chance of working out how many storeys made up the glass skyscraper that towered above them.

She looked down at the little girl's rapt expression and grinned. 'Are you looking forward to taking the lift to your dad's office, or are you scared? I'm scared. You have to promise to hold my hand and not let go.'

Actually, there was an element of truth in that remark. *Scared* might not be the right word but she was certainly nervous, and it wasn't because the lift would be whizzing them up to one of the offices in the building, but because of who would be waiting to greet them and take them both out to lunch.

After days of seeing Niccolo only in passing, he had unexpectedly arrived back to the house three hours ahead of schedule one day to find them in the kitchen, where Sophie was sitting at the table while, opposite her, Annalise worked at tracing a picture of a flower, her face scrunched up with concentration.

Sophie had looked up and there he'd been, looming in the doorway, filling it and in the act of cuffing the sleeves of his white shirt.

Her throat had gone dry, and she'd been conscious of a slow burn that spread from the inside out, firing up nerve-endings she hadn't known even existed.

What had he been thinking? It had been a hot day and he had surprised her as she'd relaxed after a morning with her little charge at Kew Gardens followed by a picnic under a spreading tree, which had been absolutely idyllic.

She'd been wearing a pair of denim shorts and a T-shirt and no bra, her hair all over the place. She'd felt grubby and she'd *looked* grubby, and even though the dark eyes that had briefly rested on her flushed face had revealed nothing, she'd taken less than two seconds to fill in the blanks and speculate at what had been going through his head.

A kid in charge of a kid.

Since she'd started working for him, Sophie had more than once berated herself for ever imagining that she might find herself in the awkward position of having to fend off unwanted advances.

When she remembered how she had practically warned him off, she cringed with embarrassment.

Memories of Scott had been in charge of her response, but even so…how on earth could she ever have imagined that someone like Niccolo Ferri would ever be tempted to behave in an inappropriate way towards her?

He was the very essence of gentlemanly decency. He was scrupulously polite without being stand-offish with her. Because he rattled her didn't mean that he was the slightest bit interested in her aside from judging her ability to look after his daughter.

He was nothing like Scott.

From nowhere, that thought flitted through Sophie's head as she held Annalise's hand and they made their way into the impressive foyer of the skyscraper.

He was nothing like Scott and she wasn't nervous now because of how he might react to her, but because of how she would react to him…

She feared her own responses, which were wildly out of sync whenever she was in his presence. Her head kept telling her how she should behave but something wayward and disobedient kept letting the side down.

She didn't want any wayward anything letting down any sides.

She didn't care if it was all down to chemistry. She didn't care that it meant nothing in the great scheme of things. What she cared about was that she should be immune to him after her miserable time with Scott.

She'd let herself trust Scott. He'd pursued her in the past but something about him, something about the fact that he seemed a little too charming and a little too good-looking and a little too sincere, had turned her off.

Then her parents had died so suddenly and, with everything around her going to pieces, she had fallen onto his sympathetic shoulder, which he had magnanimously told her she could cry on.

She had been grateful for the distraction but then, bit by bit, she had started to notice the way he had wanted to take over her life. He had seen the mess her finances had been in, her fall from grace, and he had slyly reminded her of her newly acquired far lower status amongst the peer group she had grown up with. He had become comfortable putting her down in front of them and, caught up in her own mix of sadness and confusion and misery, she had helplessly kept silent, gradually retreating from socialising, which hadn't been that difficult because friends had begun showing their true colours and retreating from her.

Maybe it had been his way of exacting some kind of revenge because she had ignored him in the past.

But gradually she had realised that that was just the person he was. His need to control was absolute and he was someone who preyed on the weak. He had issues and Sophie felt that she had escaped in the nick of time.

If anything, the experience had made her stronger and she had learnt from it, which was why, now, with butterflies in her tummy at the prospect of seeing Niccolo, she felt so irritated and frustrated with herself.

They took the lift up to his suite of offices, and Sophie wasn't sure what she had been expecting but she knew what she *should* have expected: luxury.

Still, she was unprepared for the *level* of luxury that confronted her when she emerged from the lift with Annalise attached to her like a little limpet, eyes wide and mouth open in awe.

She fiddled with the lanyard she had been given at the sprawling reception desk before they were ushered like royalty into the mirrored lift.

The expanse of pale wood seemed to go on for ever, broken by a clutch of sofas upholstered in vibrant yellow and clustered in a way that should have promoted an atmosphere of comfort and relaxation but instead made her feel a tad queasy because it was all so very elegant and picture perfect.

Beyond the furniture was a semi-circular mirrored desk, behind which two strikingly beautiful men seemed to be hard at work in front of oversized monitors.

It was a completely silent space. Beyond the foyer, the office meandered between clever glass partitions and long, low marble containers spilling over with plants. The desks were all occupied and there was the low buzz of conversation and an atmosphere of ferocious concentration and hard work.

Uninterrupted floor-to-ceiling glass drew the eye to the swirl of sky outside, and way down below, like a miniature Lego city, she could see the jagged contours of buildings and office blocks.

It was irresistible to a six-year-old. Annalise relinquished her hold of Sophie's hand, sprinting to the bank of open glass with Sophie following in hot pursuit, and they were both laughing when they were shown to Niccolo's private office space. It was up a short flight of steps, on either side of which the thin, pale railings were as delicate as a waterfall of crystal.

Nerves hit her as she saw him in his natural habitat, every inch the top dog in the cut-throat world of big money.

He wasn't formally dressed. Instead he wore charcoal trousers and a white shirt cuffed to the elbows, with no sign of a tie.

'I see Annalise has already taken herself off to see what's outside?' He half smiled and his eyes met hers over Annalise's head as he stooped down to his daughter's level to give her a brief hug. Then, as though thinking better of it, he scooped her up and carried her to the window so that she could peer outside—a bird's eye view from the top of the world.

'I couldn't stop her.'

'It's the first time she's been here.' Niccolo looked at Sophie, his expression concealed behind lush lashes.

* * *

He'd spent the past couple of days keeping their meetings brief. As distractions went, he wasn't usually open to any. Unfortunately, as distractions went, he was very much open to this particular one and he didn't like the feeling.

With all the women he dated, he knew the lie of the land. He wasn't interested in intellectual stimulation. He was interested in the business of enjoyment and so were they. He had never, to his knowledge, broken any woman's heart, and there were times when he'd seriously doubted he'd broken his ex-wife's.

He was generous to a fault when he was in a relationship. Except with his emotions. Work would always come for him, but he'd caught himself thinking about this particular woman at the most unexpected moments…during a high-level conference call…just before he switched off the light for bed…when he stopped for two seconds to gaze down absently at the view from his glass house…

Right now, she was dressed in an unalluring outfit of flowered overalls with a white T-shirt underneath and flat, tan sandals. She looked wholesome—free of make-up and extraordinarily pretty.

'You kept promising, but you were always too busy,' Annalise said, picking up the conversation after an exhaustive exploration of what the world looked like forty storeys up from every single window in Niccolo's office.

Sophie looked between them, noted the wistful look on Annalise's face and Niccolo's dark flush, and wondered how it was that he was so protective of his daughter, clearly loved her so much and yet, in some ways, was so incapable of complete engagement.

But the conversation was swept aside, carried along by Annalise, whose chatter was a buffer against any personal tangents. There were questions about everything. The eye-wateringly expensive restaurant on the thirty-first floor, with its sweeping panoramic views, was, for Annalise, *'The best place I've ever been to in my whole life...and could we come again...please...?'*

She had a photographic memory and spent some time listing every plant and flower Sophie had shown her, using their Latin names. She chatted breathlessly and with the enthusiasm of a child yearning for parental approval, and in fairness Niccolo did not stint when it came to that.

And yet...

Sophie was desperate to maintain the professionalism she knew she had to hang on to at all costs.

There was no room for curiosity, but he intrigued her, and she told herself that there was nothing wrong with that, in a way, because it was great at taking her mind off her problems. In his mansion, her frantic, depressing life seemed distant and manageable. Already bills had been cleared and what hadn't would be. There was light at the end of the tunnel and somehow, strangely, not surrounded by all the memories, she could feel her head clearing.

Her nights were becoming more peaceful, and bit by bit she felt she was finding a way to piece together her broken life so that it would once again make sense.

What was it about sharing space with a guy who got under her skin like an itch she needed to scratch that cleared her head?

After lunch she and Annalise headed back to the house, but not before Niccolo told her that he would want to chat to her after his daughter was in bed.

'I'll be late.' He had been distractedly looking at his computer as he'd spoken, propped up with his hands flat on his desk while, on the other side, Sophie could feel Annalise yawning, exhausted after the excitement of the day. When he'd glanced at her, she'd known that his mind was already somewhere else. He had had his window with them and now it was time for him to return to the business of making vast amounts of money.

'I'm in the final stages of an extremely sensitive deal and it's proving a mammoth task co-ordinating the participants to meet because they're from all over Europe.' He had smiled crookedly at her and her heart had flip-flopped madly, even though she had successfully maintained an interested but reasonably vague expression on her face. 'So, my timing is unpredictable.' He glanced at his watch and then back to her. 'Expect me back by eight-thirty, at the latest. Or is that too late for you?'

'I think I can keep my eyes open until then,' Sophie had returned politely.

'And I should have asked. Will I be interrupting any plans you might have made?'

She'd flushed because no, no plans had been made.

'I'll eat with Annalise,' she had said quickly.

'Don't be ridiculous.'

'It was a huge lunch.'

'You had an ornate salad,' he had responded drily. 'A bird would find it hard to keep going on that for the remainder of the day. I'll bring something back with me.'

And that had been the end of the conversation.

Waiting for him now, in the kitchen, Sophie felt a revival of the curiosity that had bitten into her earlier on in the day.

He'd warned her he'd be late, so she'd expected his eight-thirty to be more along the lines of nine-fifteen, but in fact she heard the sound of the front door at a little before eight and instantly all thoughts flew out of her head and every muscle in her body tensed while her nervous system went into overdrive.

She was half standing when he strode into the

kitchen, laden with various bags and bringing with him the mouth-watering aroma of Chinese food.

'I…' Her mind raced, her mouth went dry, and as always the responses she least wanted were the first to announce themselves. 'You look tired…'

'Say that again?' Niccolo stopped dead in his tracks and looked at her with his head tilted to one side. He slowly deposited the bags on the table, but his eyes were still on her and they remained there.

She looked flustered and he realised with a start that, aside from his aunt, no one usually made any kind of comments to him of that nature, and yet it was a simple enough observation and genuinely meant.

'It's been a long day,' he said eventually, breaking the silence, and sat opposite her at the kitchen table.

'But at least not as long as you'd thought. I was expecting you later.' She smiled. 'The food smells delicious.'

'You need to do it justice, so I hope you haven't eaten already…'

'Annalise ate just a little too early for me. I draw the line at five-thirty, but she could hardly keep her eyes open after all the high excitement of today. Shall I fetch some plates?'

'And two wine glasses. Join me.'

His dark eyes were thoughtful when they rested on her as she dutifully fetched the wine glasses and poured them both a glass while he began opening boxes, releasing divine aromas.

'We haven't really chatted in any great detail about how you're finding it working here, generally speaking,' he said, when she had finished bustling with the crockery and the cutlery and the glasses, notably uncomfortable at the prospect of once again having a meal with him.

Sophie glanced at him as she slowly took her place at the table. She had braided her long hair into a single plait and she absently flipped it over her shoulder and played with the end, twirling the fine, platinum blonde strands between her fingers.

'What do you mean?'

'Are you enjoying looking after Annalise? Forget about the money…are you satisfied with the work that's being asked of you?'

'Of course!' She sounded genuinely surprised at the question.

'I wouldn't want you to think that you're being asked to work too many hours, whatever you're being paid.'

'Why would you think that?' She sipped her wine and then followed his lead and began helping herself to some of the dishes in their fancy black and gold containers.

He piled into his food, drank a mouthful of wine and then proceeded to look at her over the rim of his glass. 'Because you've been nowhere since you got here, even when I've been back reasonably early in the evening—early enough for you to go out.'

Sophie stared at him. She drank some more of her wine and this time slightly more than a delicate sip. He knew his silence left no room to wriggle away from some sort of response.

'I…I'm planning on having the weekend at home to get through some more…er…clearance…'

'Maybe you could get a company to do that for you?'

'I can't. No.' She looked down and resumed eating, this time not looking at him. 'Well, I suppose I *could*,' she eventually conceded. 'I've cleared out all the bits I want to hang on to…'

'Then why don't you? Is it the cost?'

'No.' She smiled stiffly. 'Thanks to this job, I can afford it, but it seems a little wasteful to spend money for something to get done when I'm more than capable of doing it myself.'

'Thrifty.'

'I haven't had much choice. I don't suppose you'd understand.' She looked around her at the exquisite kitchen. 'Maybe *I* didn't really understand what it felt like to really have to count pennies but now I do and it's been a valuable lesson to not take anything for granted.' She half laughed and then grimaced. 'Not that you're in the slightest concerned by all of this but to get back to your question, I love being with your daughter. She's smart and very engaging. You aunt must miss being with her. How is she doing? How is your father?'

Never one to encourage girlish confidences and outpourings of heartfelt emotion, to which there was no rational response, Niccolo strangely found himself hesitating, not quite wanting to shut down the conversation just yet. He was enjoying the array of emotions that flitted across her face and the way she half toyed with her hair even when she ate, expertly wielding the wooden chopsticks provided with the meal, and the translucent violet of her eyes when she looked at him.

'What makes you think I have no idea what it feels like to be broke?' he asked, pushing his empty plate to one side and relaxing back in his chair, which he angled away from the table so that he could extend his legs, loosely crossing them at the ankles.

His eyes drifted to her mouth and it was an effort to drag them away because there was a lot to appreciate there—full lips, perfectly formed...whose imagination wouldn't shift gear?

'Do you?'

Niccolo frowned because not only had his imagination wandered into no-man's-land, but so too had the conversation.

'You don't have to answer that if you don't want to. In fact...' She stood up, reaching out to sweep the plates together, along with the boxes in which far too much had been left.

'Where are you going?' he asked irritably.

'I thought I'd tidy this stuff away and head up.'

'We haven't finished talking.'

Sophie paused. He'd asked her whether she enjoyed her job, money aside. She'd answered him. He'd felt free to pry, and she'd got the message loud and clear, but the boot was clearly not going to be put on the other foot. He asked questions, he didn't answer them.

He'd elicited information from her she hadn't shared with anyone but her curiosity about *him* wasn't going to be satisfied, so what else was there to talk about?

She lowered her eyes and kept stubbornly quiet, and when she finally looked at him there was open amusement on his face, which made her bristle.

'You can speak your mind, Sophie,' he encouraged flatly. 'This is what this conversation is all about. It's important you don't feel as though you have to stay within these four walls even when I'm here and you're technically free to go out. You must have friends you want to meet up with?'

The question hung in the air, so that she gritted her teeth and made an effort to count to ten.

'I'm fine for the moment.'

There was sudden understanding in his eyes and that felt equally offensive. He was seeing straight into the very heart of her and she didn't like it.

'I don't ask you questions about your private life,' she said tersely and then reddened at what felt like an act of insubordination, but the words had left her mouth and she didn't want to claw them back with an apology. 'I respect the fact that you don't want to impart personal information about yourself.'

'I know what it feels like to have no money,' Niccolo said quietly. 'You grew up with money and now it's gone. I grew up with none and now I have it. Both of us have had our learning curves.'

'Were your parents happy?' She tilted her head to one side and met his eyes steadily. 'I'm guessing they are now as they're still together. I'm guessing you grew up in a tightly knit family unit because Evalina is immensely close to you and to her sister and presumably to her brother-in-law.'

'Happiness isn't the be all and end all when the chips are down. There's a lot of happiness to be found in the security that comes with having deep reserves of money, enough so that you become untouchable.'

'My parents were happy,' Sophie said wistfully. 'I think it pretty much *is* the be-all and end-all even when the chips are down. I just wish I could tell them that now...' So he had grown up in poverty, and she could picture him, fiercely ambitious, contemptuous of the sordid business of never having enough, putting the learning curves in place that would make him the man he was now. But was that the whole of his story? He professed to have no time for love, but what about his wife? Maybe that was where his disillusionment stemmed from. She thought that when you lost the person you loved you probably lost your faith in happiness, and yet he had his daughter. Did he blame a childhood of having nothing for the fact that he was emotionally out of reach, or was that just a way of not dealing with the real reason, which lay in love that had been lost? He aspired to be untouchable, but really, how reasonable was that when you had a child to consider? Was that why he seemed sometimes so awkward around Annalise?

Had he ever thought to replace his ex with someone else...someone who could be a mother to Annalise?

Speculation rattled around in her head, spreading tentacles everywhere, making her wonder about him, turning him into a three-dimensional man, complex and full of depths she could feel herself wanting badly to explore.

'But moving on...'

Sophie blinked, focusing on him, wondering if she had imagined that brief lapse when he had let her past whatever iron gates he had built around himself.

'Yes.' Her voice was brisk. 'It's late.'

'There's a reason I returned home earlier than expected.'

'Oh?' She hovered, unsure whether this was a prelude to a long conversation or a brief, winding-up remark.

'I said it's been problematic getting various people together for a deal I've spent the past eight months working on.' He pushed the plates to one side and abruptly sat forward, crowding her so that she drew back a little, eyes widening.

'You mentioned that,' Sophie said vaguely.

'To expand, there's a great deal of secrecy surrounding this arrangement. It involves a family business, and my takeover has to be presented as a fait accompli to ensure that there's no loss of confidence in their market share, which would happen were there to be months of speculation about a takeover. Public knowledge that they were ready to sell would also open the door to a possible hostile takeover, which they don't want. Everything has had to be handled delicately but I have finally found a solution to all parties being present at the same time and in the same place for the details to be finalised. You might think that it's unimportant for everyone to be physically present, given the speed and efficiency of the internet and the convenience of video calls.'

'That thought hadn't crossed my mind,' Sophie said politely. 'I'm just wondering where this is all going, although, of course, I'm very happy that your deal is now finalised. That must be…er…very rewarding for you.'

'Very rewarding, and extremely lucrative,' Niccolo added drily. 'I also had no plans to disperse the hundreds of employees who currently work at the various offshoots, which is the main reason the family decided that I was the buyer they wanted.'

'That's wonderful.'

'I know what it's like,' Niccolo mused, half under his breath, 'to live at the receiving end of a company that thinks it's acceptable to get rid of someone who's given a lifetime to them because they think he's out-stayed his welcome...' He frowned, then continued without allowing room for interruption. 'At any rate, there has been insistence on the part of my client that everyone meets for the closure.' He shrugged eloquently. 'Call it an old-fashioned Italian thing... or a general mistrust on the part of an eighty-two-year-old in the workings of the internet...'

'Sometimes when you see people face to face you get a completely different opinion of them.'

'Possibly. At any rate, various family members, all of whom have shares in the company and are scat-tered in various parts of Europe, need to meet along with the discreet team of international lawyers I have put in place, and the financial and tax accountants who have done their job with admirable discretion over the months. Co-ordinating diaries has been a nightmare and more so when Evalina disappeared to Italy because there was no one to look after An-nalise.'

'That's fine.'

'Say that again?'

Sophie thought of a few days without Niccolo

around, during which she could work on getting her nervous system to a place where it didn't hive off on a dangerous tangent every single time he was around. A peaceful few days. She and Annalise could busy themselves during the day and have lovely, relaxed evenings, uninterrupted by her heartbeat picking up speed the closer to his possible arrival back at home.

She could devote her time to reminding herself just how disillusioned she was when it came to men. She could answer all those nagging emails she had tried hard to focus on before being ambushed by thoughts of her over-sexy employer.

'I'm more than happy to stay here with Annalise while you go abroad on business.' She smiled with warm reassurance. 'I hope I've proved that I'm one hundred per cent trustworthy and capable of looking after your daughter. You needn't fear that I'll be having wild parties at your house the second you board a plane!'

'No,' Niccolo murmured. 'I actually have no fears in that direction at all.'

'Good!' Sophie marvelled that he could simultaneously compliment her on her reliability and trustworthiness while in the same breath making her sound like a crashing bore with no social life.

'But I think you may have got hold of the wrong end of the stick…'

Sophie was still smiling, although there was a

little thread of apprehension filtering through her as he continued.

'I won't be leaving my daughter behind with you. Far from it. You'll both be coming with me.' He paused, giving her time to digest what he'd just announced. 'You can consider it a mini-holiday of sorts. Yes, you'll be looking after Annalise, but you'll be on board my superyacht and there will be other people around for company.'

'On board...'

'My superyacht, which is currently moored off the coast of Sardinia. I'm surprised it didn't occur to me that it would be the perfect spot to host this very private gathering, far from the reach of any snooping eyes.' He delivered a smile of complete satisfaction. 'Don't look so alarmed, Sophie; all you need is your passport, some clothes for very hot weather and, of course, as many swimsuits as you can stuff into your suitcase. My yacht comes with several extremely pleasant swimming pools...'

CHAPTER FIVE

NOTHING, NOT EVEN mixing with the kids at her fee-paying school who had come from wealthy families, could have prepared Sophie for the assault on her senses at what life looked like when you moved in the world of the uber-rich.

With back-to-back meetings before a departure date that seemed dizzyingly soon, Sophie saw precious little of Niccolo over the next three days.

He had arranged for professionals to help with the final stages of the house clearance, which had been in limbo for the past couple of weeks.

He had texted her with just a day's notice.

Friday morning at nine. I would say that I can get cover for Annalise for the day, but I have a feeling that she might enjoy the bedlam.

She did, and so did Sophie when, at a little after five on Friday, she had looked at how much had been accomplished. Not everything, but there was hardly anything left to do, with the remainder of her personal belongings all delivered to Niccolo's house, where he had assured her they could remain until her contract was over.

And, as he had predicted, Annalise had enjoyed every second of the chaos of packing and clearing, and oddly it was an exercise that had hurt far less than Sophie had expected.

Had she been subconsciously putting off the final hurdle because of the pain she had anticipated? The memories she would have had to dust down and look at?

With Annalise there and the packing men in and out and an alarming but stimulating trip staring her in the face, she had dusted down those memories but then cherished them instead of being broken up by them.

It had been fun packing for Annalise.

'Have you ever been on your dad's yacht?' she had asked as they had sifted through the sizeable wardrobe of designer summer clothes, selecting some, discarding others.

Annalise had shrugged and said, without skipping a beat and without any hint of sadness, that she hadn't.

'He doesn't come on holiday with us,' she'd explained, standing up and showing Sophie a swimsuit with frills and a pattern of fish which she exclaimed was her favourite in the whole world. 'Aunty Eva and

I go, and sometimes Daddy joins us, but he's always on his computer when he comes anyway.'

'And do you mind?' Sophie had asked casually, thinking of her own idyllic childhood with her doting parents.

'It's nice he's around more now. I liked going to see him in his office in the sky.' She had smiled and looked at Sophie with her big, dark, serious eyes. 'And it'll be nice on the boat, especially as there's a pool. Daddy has a house in the country and there's a pool there, but I only get to go with Aunty Eva for a week over summer and then Daddy comes for a week, but he prefers to be in London.'

Niccolo left ahead of them for his yacht to make sure everything was in place.

He had expanded on who would be there: the powerful Italian family, rooted in tradition, who would be able to confer as one in the same place, and six outsiders from legal and accounting professions, who would take care of all the nuts and bolts to secure the deal.

Sophie had semi-absorbed this information. She wouldn't be there to socialise. She would be there with her working hat on, whatever Niccolo might have implied to the contrary.

They would stay aboard the boat for four days while every small detail was finalised in between ensuring the clients relaxed and had some enjoyable downtime.

She decided that one sensible black swimsuit would suffice. She had several racier ones, but as she'd fished them out and looked at them they had reminded her of a time long gone and she had stuffed them in the bag of things to be donated to charity.

It was surprisingly exciting to think about having some time abroad, even if it would be of a very brief duration and even if she would be working while she was there.

She'd always loved the thrill of travelling and it was something she had foolishly never even thought about until it had been snatched away in the face of all her financial woes.

What had she expected?

The first-class flight over to Cagliari Airport, yes.

She didn't think that Niccolo would consider flying anything but First. She was still impressed, however, with just how pampered she had felt. First-class flights had always been out of her parents' league. Annalise, accustomed to nothing else, took it all for granted, amusing herself with some of the fun activity books they had bought together the day before.

What Sophie had definitely *not* expected was the limo to the airfield and then the helicopter waiting to whisk them off to his superyacht.

With the sun beating down, they had been ushered like royalty from plane to limo to a small field where a black helicopter was on standby.

Luggage had been dealt with by staff who had

been virtually invisible, taking care of every single thing so that she and Annalise had nothing to do but look around and absorb the scenery.

From the air-conditioned comfort of the limo, Sophie had gazed at the coloured houses and buildings, tightly packed together in hues of reds and yellows and oranges, climbing neatly up the hill and descending to the sea, which glittered like a jewel, dotted with the bobbing white of small boats.

Annalise gasped and squealed, her excitement making Sophie smile.

She was cool inside the limo, but the bright blue skies outside made her feel hot.

She'd worn some white jeans and a loose pink top, and wished she'd had the foresight to wear a dress instead.

The views from the limo had been beautiful, but from the buzzing helicopter the unfolding panorama was so much more spectacular.

Transported into the air and gazing down from giddy heights—while next to her Annalise clutched her hand for dear life, barely able to keep still—Sophie fell silent at the distant view of the sea, glittering and turquoise, unbelievably Technicolor-bright.

They swooped over coves nestled in steep, rocky enclaves that were lush with bushes and green with outcrops of trees.

A brief flight before the spectacle of vessels once more dotting the ocean blue preceded a sharp, giddy descent, and for a few seconds Sophie squeezed her eyes tightly shut, but not before she understood very clearly that in a sea of boats there was only one massive mothership, to which the helicopter was descending.

Niccolo wasn't the young upstart in the jungle. Niccolo was the roaring lion who sat at the top of the pecking order.

Just like that, nerves and wild anticipation replaced carefree excitement as the frantic swirl of the rotor blades stopped and the door was pushed open, and there he was, devastating in a pair of cream shorts and a faded striped T-shirt, barefoot and wearing dark sunglasses, which he immediately removed.

He moved towards them and stooped down as Annalise began running towards him before slowing to a more grown-up, sedate pace.

Sophie hovered and looked at him, and on cue he raised his dark eyes to hers above Annalise's head before vaulting upright and lifting his daughter up in one swoop that made her squeal with pleasure.

'Trip okay?' he asked, and Sophie nodded while every nerve in her body went into crazy overdrive.

How on earth could a guy look so sexy? He was the picture of bronzed, muscular beauty, his dark hair curling at the nape of his neck, his dark eyes lazy and penetrating and his wide, sensuous mouth promising untold pleasure.

The last thing Sophie wanted was to think of any

kind of pleasure with the man who was employing her to look after his daughter.

'It was great. Annalise could barely contain her excitement.' She stroked Annalise's satin-smooth cheek and was rewarded with a dimpled smile as she rested her head against her father's shoulder, clearly overjoyed at this uncustomary display of physical affection.

They began walking away from the helicopter into the bowels of the superyacht, where Sophie stood completely still and gazed around her at a vision of ridiculous luxury.

Annalise had drawn back from her comfort zone and was doing the same, but hours of travel were taking their toll and she was yawning widely, eyes staying open with difficulty.

Leather and teak and glass dominated the space. Everything was pale.

'I'll show you to your rooms.' Niccolo began moving through the living area, chatting to her about the yacht as they headed deeper down a circular flight of stairs. 'Custom-built,' he said, 'with four decks and a top speed of twenty-one knots. There's enough space for everyone coming and the crew, including two chefs. If you need anything, then you just have to ask.'

'First thing I'll need is a satnav to work my way around this. It's absolutely *massive*.'

'Never been on a yacht before?'

'Never. I don't think many people have.' She didn't quite know where to look because it was all so magnificent. 'Where is everyone?'

'Due tomorrow evening. Complex arrangements delivering them all here in various stages. Tonight, there will just be the two of us. I would include my daughter in the equation, but she's already asleep on my shoulder.'

'I…I should stay with her.' Sophie's heart sped up. She thought about them dining together and then realised that with that one thought came a spiralling cyclone of more dangerous ones. 'She'll be confused if she wakes up and she doesn't know where she is.'

Niccolo frowned. 'I could get one of my staff to sit in the adjoining room, so someone is at hand if she wakes up and is disoriented.'

'But she won't *know* whoever it is.'

'Annalise is accustomed to a variety of different people on the scene,' Niccolo said wryly. 'Evalina lives with me and is at hand ninety per cent of the time, but there's still that ten per cent when she's not around and occasionally neither am I.'

They had begun strolling through the mega-yacht. Everything was pristine. There were seating areas in places where the view of the open ocean was un-interrupted, and they walked past an entire section that included more informal seating and a bar.

'What happens when you're not using all of this?' Sophie asked, knowing that she would return to their conversation about Annalise but too distracted by her surroundings to pursue anything at the moment.

He'd grown up without much and she was beginning to realise just how ambitious he would have been and probably still was, when it came to ensuring that a life of *being without* would never be his fate. More so, she suspected, because it wasn't just about himself but about his daughter as well, about ensuring *she* had everything he had not.

But what had been sacrificed?

She slanted disobedient eyes sideways to see that Annalise was fast asleep against him, mouth half open, her long, dark lashes fluttering in sleep while he held her effortlessly with one arm. Sophie shivered as she noted the flex of muscle in his forearm, the definition of sinew and the suggestion of leashed strength.

He was a magnificent blend of grace and power and she was so busy staring that she had to drag her brain back into gear when he said, with amusement, 'Am I about to get a telling off?'

Sophie smiled, relaxing at the teasing lightness in his voice. 'It seems a waste if it's just left here bobbing about on the water, waiting for you to pop in for a visit now and again to make sure the engine's still ticking over and there are no cobwebs on the decks.'

Niccolo burst out laughing then stifled his laughter as Annalise shifted against him, her eyes fluttering open for a few seconds.

'You have a colourful way with words, Sophie,' he whispered.

She realised she quite liked the way he said her name, as soft and sensory as the brush of a feather against her skin.

'Well, you have to admit that it's an awfully big toy for a rich guy.' She glanced sideways to the view of a lavender sky announcing the end of day. 'Do you have people on board all the time even when it's not being used?'

'If I said yes,' Niccolo drawled, with a thread of laughter still there in his voice, 'would I get a few brownie points for alleviating any unemployment problems in this part of the world?'

'No!'

'That's very harsh. Up this flight of stairs is the master suite and two adjoining rooms that have prime position with excellent views of the ocean from all angles. I have arranged for us to occupy these quarters.'

Suddenly the mega-yacht seemed to shrink to the size of a matchbox.

How private could bedrooms be on a yacht, however big the yacht was?

Big enough, she discovered seconds later, to accommodate a suite for Niccolo and mini-suites for her and Annalise, each with generously proportioned bathrooms. They were connected by a sitting area where they could all relax.

It was the last word in luxury and yet all that occupied Sophie's mind was the fact that Niccolo's room was directly opposite, and to make matters worse he inserted, casually, 'If you need anything, you just have to knock on my door, or...' he nodded to a small gadget on the wall by the thick glass window that looked out on a dazzling view of sea '...that will summon someone.' He nudged open one of the doors that led to the smaller of the rooms and gently deposited his daughter on the bed, which was beautifully made up with just the sort of brightly patterned linen that a child would love. 'For now, we will have dinner brought to us here. That way Annalise will have familiar faces around her if she wakes unexpectedly, although it's my experience that being on this size yacht on calm water is actually very conducive to sleep.'

Sophie, still playing with myriad images of him sleeping in his own quarters practically within touching distance, nodded vaguely and watched, eyes glazed, as he settled Annalise.

'You're hovering,' he pointed out, helpfully. 'Your luggage will already be in your bedroom. Why don't you unpack while I organise something for us to eat?'

He was already pulling out his mobile phone, which was probably the most efficient way of contacting his chief steward on a yacht the size of a small town.

'Go on,' he urged, looking at her with amusement,

'feel free to shower and change if you want. I'll wait here just in case Annalise wakes up. Then we can eat, and you can tell me how wasteful I am having a yacht this size and I can defend myself.'

He grinned, and just like that Sophie was swept away on a rush of something warm and uncomfortable and alarming. It was as though all those nebulous responses had finally coalesced into a pool of hot, naked attraction that made her heart leap with frenzied panic and brought a surge of hot colour to her cheeks.

He was teasing her. For a moment, she saw past that remote, powerful, charismatic stranger to someone utterly charming and insanely sexy.

And her body was reacting like the young, redblooded woman she thought she had safely confined to deep freeze after all the business with Scott.

Dampness pooled between her legs and she had to resist the urge to squirm. Her breasts, pushing against her cotton bra, felt heavy, and her nipples were stiff and sensitive.

She was horrified because all she could think was, *I want them to be touched...played with...sucked... by this man.*

She almost put her hand to her mouth in shock.

'I'll unpack,' she said on a deep breath, 'but I'll leave the shower for later. And there's no need to justify why you own this lovely yacht.' Her brain had cranked back into gear and was shrieking that the only defence against this unwelcome attraction was to make sure she didn't lose sight of the fact that theirs was a working relationship.

He was her boss.

He gave the orders and she obeyed.

There was a little bit of socialising but that was to be expected. In short, there were lines that were not to be crossed and she was upset with herself for looking at those lines and then stepping over them.

She fled to the safety of her bedroom, keenly aware of him outside, metres away.

It was huge, with a double bed beautifully made up in deep burgundy linen, exquisitely soft to the touch. The carpet was thick and plush, and everything was fitted, seamlessly blending together in shades of pale wood, from the bedside cabinets to the generous bank of wardrobes nestled around a sleek dressing table. The bathroom was even bigger than the bedroom and she was briefly tempted to actually do as Niccolo had suggested and have a shower, but instead she unpacked quickly, more to give herself a bit of breathing space than because there was any need to actually hang anything up.

About to head outside, she paused to look in the mirror above the dressing table.

She looked flustered. Her cheeks were pink, and she placed both hands on them in an attempt to cool the heat. She had tied her hair back, but now she neatened it because she looked tousled when she wanted to look prim and professional. Her eyes were bright—too bright—and when she squinted at her reflection she felt she could detect the very slightest quiver in her body, as though she was plugged into a socket and was quietly vibrating, engine fired up and ready to go.

She gritted her teeth, hating herself for her lack of control, and pushed open the door to the outside living area to find Niccolo sprawled in one of the cream leather chairs, feet crossed at the ankles, the very picture of a billionaire at rest.

'I've ordered a selection of salads,' he announced, his dark eyes resting on her face, watching as she primly sat on the sofa facing him.

Not even the non-stop stress of constant travel, he mused, could detract from her delicate, captivating beauty. He didn't want to look but he couldn't seem to stop himself. She moved with the grace of a dancer, blushed like a virgin even as she tilted her head in absolute defiance if she disagreed with him…and was she aware of how sexy she looked when she inclined her head to one side and parted her lips and did a little frown as she thought about something he'd said?

Playing with fire had never felt so tempting. He enjoyed watching the flit of emotions skittering across her face, and he really liked the way she reacted when he dumped the work hat and wrongfooted her by talking to her as any man talking to a woman, without the business of anyone being in anyone's pay.

He couldn't remember experiencing anything like this before. When he thought of his wife and their brief courtship, he realised that what he'd felt then had certainly not been this strange playfulness that wanted to get a reaction. He thought of Caroline and remembered the formality and sophistication of those few months before he had proposed. They had been an elegant couple moving amongst their elegant crowd, cocooned by wealth and power, the very wealth and power he had striven for all of his life but which had somehow felt hollow and empty when he was married, as though something vital had been missing.

He surely couldn't recall this simple enjoyment of looking and musing and imagining. Was it because he knew that nothing would come of it? Or was it simply a case of a change being as good as a rest? Shy, ethereal blondes who didn't play games versus bold brunettes who held nothing back?

'Yummy.'

'Of course, if you'd rather something else…'

'A salad would be fine,' Sophie said politely.

'You can relax, Sophie,' Niccolo said with a disgruntled edge. 'Tell me how much more you have to do with your house. Has it been completely cleared?'

'Mostly.'

'And…how do you feel now? About that?' He

was taking steps down that previously taboo road of encouraging an emotional response and he realised that this was becoming something of a habit as far as this woman was concerned. Curiosity was trumping common sense, but instead of being wary he felt invigorated. His palate had become jaded, and it was thrilling being unexpectedly presented with an opportunity to dust it down and take it for a walk. Who would be able to resist the temptation?

It would seem, he mused, that money didn't buy everything after all.

Sophie sighed. She thought of her family home quietly and efficiently being stripped of its soul as personal effects were boxed up or given to charity or sold to help clear debts.

Suddenly everything had happened faster than the speed of light, which, she now reflected, wasn't a bad thing. It had been easy to fall into the trap of struggling to find a way forward.

Why was it so tempting to pour her heart out to this guy?

'You can talk to me,' Niccolo urged softly.

'Stop being so persuasive,' she responded with helpless honesty and he smiled, long and slow, thrilling her to the core and killing off the bit of her that was so keen to keep distance between them. If he chose to breach the distance and close the gap, then it was just so hard not to yield.

'I'm normally not,' Niccolo admitted, and she frowned.

'What do you mean?' She gazed at him and then said, in a low voice, 'Ah, I understand. You don't want anyone trespassing and the best way to stop that is to never take down the *Keep Out* signs.'

'I'm not sure I would describe it like that...'

Sophie didn't say anything, but she wondered whether he was aware of the compliment he had just inadvertently paid her. Did he feel that it was different encouraging her to talk to him about stuff that mattered because she *worked* for him? Because she posed no threat when it came to emotional involvement?

In one fell swoop he had established the door that stood between them even though it felt as though he had opened it, allowing her to see what was inside.

'I feel,' she said truthfully, 'as though sorting the house out is something that's been a long time coming. I thought it would have been so huge that subconsciously I'd put it off even though, naturally, with people moving in, I would have had to focus and get on with it eventually, but somehow...'

'Somehow?'

'It's been good to have taken my time sorting through things...not being rushed into doing anything hasty...maybe getting rid of anything I might have later regretted getting rid of...'

'You're too young,' Niccolo murmured with heartfelt sincerity, 'to have had to cope with events that could have overwhelmed you. Is that when you made your mistake?'

'What are you talking about?'

Was he opening a can of worms?

She'd been through a tough time…so yes, he'd encouraged her to open up and he couldn't beat himself up over that because she was in charge of his daughter and it made sense that he get to know her on a more personal basis than an employee in his company. But asking her about her love life…about her sex life…was that a step too far?

Yet he wanted to cross whatever lines should or shouldn't be crossed. For the very first time in his life.

There was no way he would ever, *could* ever, *not* exert complete control over himself, over his decisions, but for the moment, relinquishing control felt like a good option. Everyone needed to take a break now and again and, as breaks went, they didn't come safer than this.

'The guy who broke your heart.'

Of course, he knew that she wasn't going to give him an answer, but he was still taken aback when she said, recovering fast from her confidences of only moments ago, 'You should tell me what my duties are while I'm on board your yacht. I know I'll be in charge of Annalise, but we won't be able to do our

usual things and I'm guessing you'll want to make
sure your deal-making isn't interrupted too much by
the presence of your daughter.'

'Have you always been as private as you are?'

'Have you always found it hard to let yourself go?'

'In actual fact,' Niccolo murmured huskily, 'I'm
exceedingly good at letting myself go, given the right
circumstances...'

He looked at her with lazy, brooding eyes, skew-
ering her to the chair and obliterating all thought
from her head.

Of course she knew what he was saying!

Was he aiming to shock?

Did her reticence challenge him, somehow? She
suspected that perhaps it did. Maybe he enjoyed rus-
tling her feathers. He was a man who had everything,
and sometimes people who had everything took pleasure in finding those small things they didn't have.

Like a nanny in his employ who reacted to everything he said without being able to help herself...a
girl who had never quite learnt how to flirt, despite
mixing in groups where that was the norm. A girl
who, face it, had been slightly out of her depth at her
expensive private school, too bookish and too shy,
despite her looks, to cultivate the veneer of easy ar-
rogance that so many of her peers had had.

Her parents had been too protective for her to really ever know what it felt like to be free to do ex-

actly what she wanted without caring whether she disappointed them or not.

Did he find something amusing about the fact that she was at odds with her accent?

And yet, he had told her that his background was far from wealthy. Did he now surround himself with the sort of women a life of crazy money had opened up to him?

She lowered her eyes, her long lashes concealing her expression, but she could feel the heavy thudding of her heart at the graphic images his throwaway teasing rejoinder had kickstarted inside her.

'I've made you uncomfortable,' Niccolo said huskily. 'I apologise.'

'You enjoy making me uncomfortable.' Sophie looked at him, clear eyed, her violet gaze unwavering.

'Strangely,' he raised his eyebrows, his dark eyes locking with hers, 'I find you have a similar effect on me whether you enjoy it or not.'

The silence stretched and stretched until Sophie could almost hear it humming between them.

She licked her lips and this time the fire that was suddenly blazing between them was so hot that Niccolo could almost reach out and touch it.

Was she aware of it?

If *she* wasn't, then he certainly was, and suddenly it no longer felt like an amusing game.

What the hell was going on?

He breathed in sharply, but it was the deferential knock on the door that severed the connection.

Food. How long had someone been trying to get their attention?

He vaulted upright, relieved when the young lad bowed his way into the suite, taking far too long to explain what salads had been prepared and apologising profusely because he should have been there ten minutes ago, but he was a new member of the crew and had yet to fully familiarise himself with the layout of the yacht.

Niccolo allowed him to ramble on for a while because it was preferable to returning to violet eyes that seemed capable of doing all sorts of uninvited things to his peace of mind.

Eventually, he waved the boy out and quietly shut the door behind him before turning to Sophie.

'Help yourself.'

Everything was spread on a double-tiered chrome and glass trolley, including a bottle of wine, which Niccolo felt it prudent to steer clear of.

He helped himself to what was there and out of the corner of his eye noted every detail of her slender hands as she scooped salad onto a plate. The very fair, downy hair on them, the length of her fingers and the blunt practicality of her short nails. He could just about catch a glimpse of her blonde hair escaping around her face in untidy tendrils and he could hear her soft breathing as she concentrated on what she was putting on her plate.

He told her what she was expected to do, and he was aware of her answering, her voice low. How had he failed to realise just how pleasing it was to the ear?

Yes, she would make sure Annalise was entertained, but she was here to work and not play...

Were things back to normal?

He damn well hoped so.

Eyes carefully averted, Sophie heard herself relentlessly chattering her way through the meal. The salads were delicious. She ignored the wine, as did he, and instead washed everything down with bottled water.

His eyes were on her, lazy and assessing. She suspected he was probably bored witless with her non-stop twittering, but she was desperate to break a silence that seemed suddenly fraught.

As soon as she had eaten the last of what she thought was an acceptable amount of the fantastically prepared food, she politely pushed her plate to one side and began standing up.

Only then did she risk looking at him.

He too was rising to his feet—so tall, so aggressively masculine...and so close to her... Far too close, close enough to set her heart thumping a panicked tattoo, close enough for her to stumble back a few inches.

Close enough for her to see, with alarm, panic and dark, forbidden excitement, her own dangerous desire mirrored in his lazy, brooding gaze.

After half an hour of ceaseless wittering, she could find no words to break the thick, electric silence. It wrapped around them until breathing became difficult.

'No,' she finally croaked. She realised that somehow they had closed the gap between them. She realised that *somehow* her hand was resting on the washboard hardness of his stomach. She could feel him breathing and it was as if they had suddenly become bonded, his energy flowing into her, energising her and terrifying her at the same time.

'No,' Niccolo echoed thickly. He stepped back, breaking the spell but not so much that she could tear her eyes away from him. The drag on her senses made her weak, weak with a fierce longing she hadn't known she possessed.

Loneliness, she thought wildly. Stress and loneliness, and there he had been, the last guy she could ever possibly go for, and all that stress and loneliness had found refuge in him because, whatever stupid attraction she felt, she was inherently safe.

'I'm tired. I need to go to sleep. I'll see you... *Annalise* and I will see you in the morning.' She knew that she was stumbling over her words.

Staring at him, she was ashamed that she wanted to see more of what she had seen before, more of that burning desire, but he stepped back as well and looked down for a few seconds, shielding his expression, and then when he lifted his eyes they were cool and controlled and she wondered whether she had imagined the past five intense, scorching minutes.

He didn't say anything, except to tell her that someone would collect the dishes within the next half an hour, then with a nod he was gone, and she sagged like a puppet, strings abruptly cut.

What had just happened? She didn't quite know, but she *did* know that it was not going to happen again.

CHAPTER SIX

NOT EVEN SIMMERING tension and a sickening sense of needing to be on guard at all times could detract from the magnificence of her surroundings.

The following day was a busy one, with Niccolo's clients arriving in stages, some by the very same helicopter that had transported her and Annalise to the yacht, others by speedboats, one of which was a dedicated speedboat that seemed to be stored somewhere within the vast hull of the yacht.

Because of the number of decks on the yacht, all of which overlooked the main entry point, Sophie and Annalise could keep a safe distance while they both watched the comings and goings, fascinated. There was a sense of urgency in the air, which even Annalise felt because she couldn't quite focus on any of the fun activities Sophie had planned for the day.

The sun was beautifully warm, even in the shade where they both lounged on sofas that perched by one of three outdoor pools, this one small but with a lovely jacuzzi to one side. They could hear the distant sound of voices carrying on the warm air up to where they sat.

They had been shown to the pool area first thing by one of the many members of staff, and several hours later that very same member of staff had been their self-appointed waiter in residence, bringing them drinks and lunch and hovering to make sure their every need was met with speed.

They had swum and done some arts and crafts, and for a couple of hours they had watched a bit of television and then eaten at the private dining area just off the pool area.

And Niccolo? It was a little after four in the afternoon and Sophie had not laid eyes on him yet. She had finally stopped glancing surreptitiously in all directions, like a spy in a B-rated movie, and was just beginning to relax, back at the pool, when she was alerted to Niccolo's presence by Annalise.

He was behind her and she froze for a few seconds, then turned around, her smile in place, the lectures she had given herself during the course of the day echoing in her ears.

The modest black swimsuit she wore suddenly felt like a thong bikini as she rose fluidly from the padded deckchair, swiftly wrapping her sarong around her waist while Niccolo was distracted by his daughter.

'Had a good day?' He glanced at her for a few seconds from the kneeling position he had adopted to look at his daughter's sketchpad, and then stood up to move to one of the chairs next to where Sophie had been sitting moments earlier.

Suddenly roused from her natural tiredness after having spent most of the day outside in the sun, Annalise was now bright-eyed and bushy-tailed and desperate to commandeer her father's attention.

Still in her swimsuit, she proceeded, for the next ten minutes, to proudly demonstrate her swimming prowess until, laughing, Niccolo stood up and started unbuttoning his loose white linen shirt.

Sitting ramrod-straight on the deckchair and hiding behind sunglasses, Sophie watched in fascinated horror at what looked like the beginnings of a striptease.

Off came the linen shirt and her mouth went dry at the sight of a body not even her wildest flights of imagination could have done justice to. Broad shoulders rippled with muscle. His nipples, flat and brown, were small discs accentuating his pecs. His stomach was flat, the perfect six-pack tapering to a narrow waist. He had just the right amount of body hair to advertise in no uncertain terms that he was all male…all glorious, unashamedly and outrageously sexy alpha male.

The shorts were now coming off. Sophie held her breath. Underneath, he was wearing swimming trunks, loose and silky and riding low. Made sense.

He was on his yacht surrounded by the ocean. No better place to be prepared for getting wet.

She realised that she was still holding her breath and still gaping as he stepped into the pool. It wasn't big enough for fancy diving, but she suspected that if it had been he would have executed something pretty impressive.

He was beautiful. He moved with the grace of a panther and was compelling to look at. Thank goodness he was too busy swimming with Annalise, allowing her to clamber onto his shoulders so that she could splash with spluttering laughter into the water, to notice that he had become prime spectator fodder for Sophie.

She tore her avid gaze away with difficulty and was busily staring at a jumble of words in her book, pretending to read, when she became aware of his shadow looming over her.

'You didn't want to join us?'

Sophie looked up at him through her dark sunglasses and plastered a rictus smile on her face. Once in that forced position, her jaw began to ache, but she couldn't seem to assume a normal expression because she was too aware of him right there in front of her greedy gaze, all wet and lean and sinfully, sinfully sexy.

Annalise, wrapped in one of the oversized beach towels that had been brought for them, had plonked herself on the deckchair and was lying down, eyes closed, a little smile on her face.

'Sophie's been teaching me how to do handstands in the pool,' she said, without opening her eyes.

'Maybe she could teach me,' Niccolo said, his dark eyes not leaving Sophie's face for a single second. 'It's been a dream of mine...'

'Has it really?' Sophie said drily. She drew her knees up and wrapped her arms around them, and then stared out to sea.

The yacht had moved during the course of the day, although the sailing had been so smooth that she had barely noticed, and land was now a distant slither, a dark strip far off into the blue horizon. All around them, the ocean was still and dark, gently lapping the steep sides of the yacht.

'Where are all your...er...guests?'

'Busying themselves relaxing and then getting ready for a three-course meal,' Niccolo said as he sat on the chair next to her and laid back, mimicking his daughter, arms folded and legs lightly crossed at the ankles.

Sophie felt a little telltale tic at the side of her mouth, a giveaway sign of the strain of keeping her eyes averted when her whole body was reminding her of how vitally aware she was of his presence inches away from her.

He was a burnished, healthy bronze, and alongside him she felt translucently pale.

'I've asked the lovely guy who's been taking care of us all day to bring us an early supper in the room.'

Niccolo opened his eyes to slits and slid them across to Sophie.

She'd been in his head off and on throughout the day. He'd found himself actively resisting the temptation to seek her out on the pretext of making sure she and Annalise were okay even though he knew they would be. He had given appropriate instructions to the head of staff to know that their every need would have been met.

He had held out because surely the magnitude of this deal overrode any inexplicable desire to see what his nanny and Annalise were up to?

But now...

He had taken one look at her in that swimsuit over which she had hastily flung a sarong and the libido he had sternly reprimanded the evening before had promptly decided to break free and run wild.

The sun was already beginning to turn her skin a pale gold and bleach her hair to an even more impossible shade of white-blonde, and those dark-lashed violet eyes, resting briefly on him as he'd made his appearance, had detonated a series of explosive images that had forcibly reminded him just how easy it was for her to wreak havoc with his prized self-control.

She'd hidden away behind some oversized sunglasses and that had been frustrating because he'd been desperate to read the expression on her face.

For the first time in his life, Niccolo had reluctantly been forced to acknowledge that he was interested in a woman who didn't seem disposed to return the favour.

Did she fancy him? He was sure she did. He'd read it in her eyes the evening before, had felt that swift intake of breath and noted the way she had moved towards him, their combined heat suddenly turning the space between them into a furnace until he'd broken the connection.

Thankfully, she had stepped back at the same time, as keen as he had been to move away from a potentially awkward situation.

That said…

Niccolo realised that he'd grown to take it as a given that a woman, in receipt of any show of positive encouragement from him, would pursue him even if he'd had a change of mind.

Since when, he thought wryly, had he become such a spoiled brat when it came to the opposite sex? Had he reached a place where he stamped his feet if a woman he happened to fancy decided to give him the cold shoulder? In this case, the cold shoulder was *precisely* what was needed!

He should have been breathing a sigh of heartfelt relief that he wasn't in the position of having to deflect unwanted attention! Or worse…sack his aunt's friend for inappropriate behaviour.

Far from breathing any sighs of relief, however, Niccolo was frowning, already deciding that he would make sure whoever was at hand to wait on them the following day was not a young, red-blooded guy who would not be able to resist Sophie's obvious appeal.

'There's no need,' he drawled now, 'to be cooped up in your quarters with Annalise for the duration of the night. Every single member of my staff has been vetted and the majority are permanent employees on this yacht as well as at my villa in Costa Smeralda. I know several who would be delighted to help out with Annalise so that you have a bit more freedom of movement while you're here.'

'I'm not here to have freedom of movement,' Sophie said, turning to him with some consternation. 'I'm here to look after Annalise. That's my job.'

Niccolo didn't reply. Instead he lazily reached down to where he had tossed the shorts he'd worn over his swimming trunks and pulled out his mobile phone to make a quick call. Within minutes, a young woman, introduced as Julia, was on deck with them. She was smartly uniformed with dark hair tied back and a pleasant, friendly face.

Niccolo told her what he wanted, and Sophie listened in mounting dismay as she heard him instruct the young woman to take over.

Annalise was flagging and seemed content enough to head off with Julia, who, it transpired, she had actually met some while back when she and Evalina had gone to Niccolo's villa for a holiday.

'She might show you something special if you're good…' he said as he smiled at his daughter.

'What?' Annalise had sprung to her feet, eyes immediately bright.

'You'll see. Word of warning, though…' He was still smiling, and Annalise had moved to stand to attention in front of him, hands behind her back. 'Fifteen minutes of play there and then it's dinner for you and bed. It's been a long day.'

'Will you…?' She hesitated. 'Would you listen to me read for a bit? I've started a new book with Sophie…'

Keeping to the background, Sophie smiled and gave her small charge an encouraging nod and a thumbs-up sign. She'd forgotten that this was something they had chatted about a couple of days ago. Having observed his hesitancy in being hands-on, which seemed so strangely at odds with his keen sense of protectiveness for his daughter, she had figured it was a good idea to help encourage more time together to help rebuild their bond.

Just thinking along those lines calmed her, enabled her to shove to one side the intrusion of physical responses she didn't want.

'She's doing brilliantly with her reading,' Sophie added warmly. 'She's started a book I can remember reading when I was her age. You're enjoying it, aren't you, Annalise?'

Annalise was nodding with enthusiasm while Sophie wondered how she would spend the remainder of the evening if Julia was going to take over night duties.

The yacht was so large that there was no end to places she could explore, but of course the last thing Niccolo would want would be for her to keep popping up like an annoying jack-in-the-box wherever he happened to be with his clients.

He answered her question before she had had time to mull it over in depth by saying, sotto voce as he headed off with Annalise grasping his hand just in case he chose to wander off, 'I would very much like you to join us for dinner tonight, Sophie. There will be a total of fourteen people and it'll all be very informal, so...' he looked at her wryly '...no need to worry about not having the right thing to wear. A pair of shorts and a T-shirt will do the trick.'

'But...'

'Drinks at six-thirty and dinner to be served at seven-thirty.'

'But won't you want to discuss business...to work?'

'Today has been very successful on the "discuss-
ing business" front.' Niccolo shot her a slow, curling
smile that made her think that he could read every
objection racing to the surface in her head and would
be keen to discuss each and every one of them. 'So
it's all about relaxing this evening. It won't be a late
one. The head of the clan likes his early nights. I'll
knock on your door at six-fifteen. Doesn't give you
a huge amount of time to play with but, like I said,
there's no dress code, so just wear the first thing that
comes to hand.'

And that was the end of the conversation.

In a hurried daze, Sophie took the opportunity to
grab some clothes while Annalise was being shown
whatever surprise she had been promised. Then she
raced through a shower, using the facilities by the
pool, where everything was at hand, including towels and shampoos and scented body wash, all in a
space that was as luxurious as the most expensive
scented spa. It was preferable to jostling for space
in her quarters, where Niccolo would be bonding
and Julia would be hovering, waiting to take over.

She had five minutes to kill before a knock on the
door signalled Niccolo's arrival.

Sophie immediately tensed, breathed in deeply
and pulled open the door.

She had put on a navy-blue button-down dress with
a pattern of tiny white flowers and cap sleeves. It

was figure-hugging to the waist and then flared to just above the knee. And she had left her hair loose, for once, a tangle of curls that reached almost to her waist.

Nothing could have prepared Niccolo for the assault to his senses brought on by the sight of her. He sucked in a sharp, shaky breath and for a few seconds his mind went completely blank.

He had such a sudden, powerful urge to reach out and touch this sweetly forbidden fruit that he shoved his hands deep into the pockets of his loose grey linen trousers.

'You're ready,' he said gruffly. 'Most women I've met find it impossible to get their act together in under two hours.'

'And even more women would be insulted at that sweeping generalisation.' Sophie half turned to gather a small string bag then spun round to see him grinning as he backed towards the door to nudge it open with his shoulder before stepping aside to let her precede him out.

'None of the ones I've ever dated.' He was still grinning, his dark eyes sliding appreciatively over her as she looked ahead, chin tilted, mouth pursed in righteous indignation. He wanted nothing more than to kiss it back into a smile.

He gave up trying to fight an urge that felt too powerful for him. Sometimes, he thought, it might actually be a good thing to release some of that rigidly held self-control which defined his behaviour.

It had certainly worked when it came to Annalise, he now thought. Hadn't it? He'd never been so relaxed around his daughter before. He'd stopped being the father whose job it was to provide and protect and allowed himself to be the father who also had fun. Or at least he was getting there.

Sophie muttered something but he didn't quite catch it.

'What?'

She followed as he led them through the yacht and the myriad nooks and crannies for sitting and relaxing and socialising and eating, all a marvel of sophisticated leather and glass and metal combinations interspersed with rugs and expensive artefacts.

'I *meant* that I'd bet every one of those women you dated could get ready in under fifteen minutes if they had to,' Sophie said tartly.

'Then why do I always end up looking at my watch whenever I arrange to meet them somewhere?'

'I hear that nothing beats a fashionably late entrance.'

'Do you use that gimmick when it comes to impressing a man?'

Instead of her hackles rising, and maybe it was the effects of a day spent lazing in the sun by a pool with someone waiting on her hand and foot, but she couldn't get annoyed. She said on a groan, 'Are you about to invade my private life again?'

'I wouldn't dream of it,' Niccolo murmured.

'Wouldn't you?' she returned drily, breath hitching in her throat as she glanced across at him.

'You've already warned me off asking questions you don't want to answer—'

'And you often obey when people warn you not to do something? You never, *ever* just ignore them and power ahead regardless?'

'I'm very much liking this new-style Sophie,' Niccolo said in a low, amused voice which managed to be serious enough for Sophie to feel a tingle of delicious danger thread through her. 'Can I see a bit more of her? She's a lot more intriguing than the one who's on guard all the time.'

Sophie became aware of the low murmur of voices ahead of them, but strangely she wished they could carry on talking. His sexy drawl was sending pleasurable shivers through her and she was sick of being on the defensive around him.

'I'm on guard for a reason,' Sophie murmured, half to herself, thinking about Scott and the way she had walked through a door she should never, ever have walked through because, for a moment in time, she had been so vulnerable after her parents' death.

'Tell me…'

But it was the wrong time and the wrong place,

Niccolo knew, for this conversation and it was one he would return to.

She intrigued him and he had given up trying to either analyse or justify his reactions.

Ahead of them, duty called. This was what he was about. Duty and work first. This was what he had spent his entire adult life striving for and his entire teenage life aiming to achieve…financial security on such a scale that he became untouchable.

For once, duty felt onerous, but for the next three hours he complied, even though his eyes kept straying and his thoughts kept playing around with all sorts of contraband scenarios.

She circulated with grace and ease, comfortable chatting to whomever she happened to be with. No one would ever guess that this was a woman who had been through a year and a half of trauma and was only on this yacht at all because circumstances had forced her hand, because she had needed the money on offer.

Was it a background at private school that had accomplished that? No, he surmised. She was simply someone who didn't put herself ahead of the crowd, despite the way she looked. She was happy to listen, and a good listener was usually excellent when it came to putting people at ease.

His ex-wife had had a tendency to dominate proceedings. All eyes had to be focused on her. She had been raised to expect adulation, and the women he had dated since then? Lush, raven-haired beauties who knew how to flirt but would have been at sea amidst this sort of crowd, where the gentle ebb and flow of conversation they would have found too highbrow and probably boring as hell.

But Sophie…

Niccolo found himself itching to pick up the conversation where they had left off and he did, the moment the last of the guests had retired to their various cabins.

'As bad as you imagined it was going to be?'

They had left the table at a little after eleven. Now, walking slowly through the yacht, Sophie felt a lazy sense of contentment.

'I never thought it was going to be an ordeal,' Sophie returned. 'I'm accustomed to…well, entertaining, I guess. Cocktail-party small talk. Mixing and mingling with people you know you're not likely to see very much of again. My dad…' Her breath caught in her throat and she swallowed hard. 'My parents used to do quite a bit of entertaining back in the day, and they always encouraged me to take part.'

'Proud of you, no doubt,' Niccolo mused, 'and for good reason.'

Sophie blushed and kept her eyes averted, but she was too alert to his presence alongside her to be aware of anything else, including the hushed elegance of her surroundings. 'I made small talk.' She shrugged. 'It's not exactly the same as winning the Nobel Peace Prize or finding a cure for cancer.'

Niccolo burst out laughing. 'Join me on the upper deck,' he urged. He looked down at her, his dark eyes warm and amused, and Sophie blushed even more. 'It's not that late. A nightcap? Before the coach turns back into a pumpkin and Cinderella has to flee the ball?'

His soft laugh felt like a challenge and Sophie thought that there was surely no harm in chatting to him for another half an hour or so. She was all wound up after a night of socialising, which was something she hadn't done in a very long time. Was it selfish to want to feel normal again? Was it wrong to want to indulge in the heady and perfectly natural glow of having a conversation with a handsome guy? It was hardly as though anything was going to go anywhere, but she felt as if she'd spent so long with the weight of the world on her shoulders, feeling weary and old before her time.

'Maybe a quick nightcap,' she said in a rush, before she had time to change her mind.

'You won't regret it. There's nothing quite as spectacular as the view of an ocean at night when you're in the middle of it.'

He led the way. The stillness around them felt impossibly intimate and Sophie gasped when they emerged out onto the upper deck and the balmy night air, salty and aromatic, wrapped itself around her.

Above, the sky was velvety black, studded with infinite stars. She moved to stand by the railing and breathed in the night air. Into the distance, the ocean was as dark as a vast inkwell, softly rising and falling, breathing gently all around them.

And the silence was so profound that she could hear the smallest sound of the ocean lapping against the hull of his massive yacht.

Niccolo moved to stand right next to her, hands also on the railings, both of them staring out to sea.

'You're right,' Sophie said into the silence, her voice hushed and awed, 'it *is* spectacular. Out here… it's an amazing feeling being adrift on the ocean.'

Niccolo didn't say anything. He looked sidelong at her, appreciating the tilt of her head and the way her eyes were half closed as she absorbed her surroundings. He angled his body round so that he was now leaning against the railing, elbows over the side, and he continued to stare at her for a few more seconds, before saying casually, 'So you were going to tell me why you're on guard all the time…'

'Was I?' But she wasn't on guard now. She was ridiculously relaxed and just a little bit pleasantly heady after a couple of glasses of champagne and fine food and pleasant company. She turned to face him.

The breeze, still close and warm even at this time of the evening, blew her fine hair this way and that and the summer dress billowed ever so slightly, and Niccolo discovered what it felt like to have trouble breathing.

To have trouble getting his thoughts straight.

'You were,' he said in a strangled voice. He couldn't peel his eyes from her delicate face, upturned as she gazed at him. The ache in his groin was so uncomfortable he had to adjust his stance, and just like that he thought about no longer fighting this inexplicable urge he had to let desire call the shots.

If she pushed him away, if she managed to cling on to enough sanity for the two of them, then so be it. He would back off at a rate of knots, and in fact, maybe it would be a *good* thing if she told him to get lost.

He stared down at her, then he reached out and stroked the side of her face with his knuckle. Her skin was satin-smooth and he felt her breathe in sharply and still.

'Niccolo…'

'Tell me to stop, Sophie, and I'll stop. Immediately. No questions asked.' His voice was unsteady, his craving reaching fever-pitch as she started to breathe rapidly, and soft temptation drifted in the air between them. 'This will never be mentioned again, but, Sophie…I want you. I want to make love to you.'

CHAPTER SEVEN

TERRIBLE IDEA. The words rang through Sophie's head, strident and imperious and demanding she call a halt to this.

He was her boss! And she was sworn off men! She'd made a promise to herself that she wouldn't dip her toes into matters of the heart until she had sorted herself out…and when she did, *if* she ever did, then she would use cool judgement to ensure she never made another mistake again. She would never allow another Scott to worm his way into her life.

But her feverish mind was playing second fiddle to her even more feverish body and she knew that her breathing had become sluggish, and her eyes remained treacherously riveted to his dark, unbearably handsome face.

She reached out to gently push him back, to create some desperately needed space between their bodies, but found her hand remained on his stomach, and after a couple of seconds he covered her hand with his and then stroked it, rolling his finger over her knuckles, which elicited a soft moan from her.

Sophie closed her eyes and tiptoed up, inviting his kiss. Still, the touch of his lips against hers sent a rush of blood to her head and she almost swayed. She reached to clutch his shirt and took a step towards him, eyes still closed, not breaking their contact, just loving the feel of his tongue against hers, wet and hungry.

She was close enough to feel the prominent bulge in his shorts and moaned again.

The air was warm and sultry and the stillness of the dark night around them seemed to lock them into a bubble where the only sounds were the telltale noises of two people craving more.

And how long would they have remained there, locked in their embrace?

Would they have somehow found themselves making out like a couple of horny teenagers by the side of the pool?

At what point would one of them have woken up to the madness of what they were doing?

Neither had the chance because they were interrupted by a soft cough from somewhere behind them.

It was so soft that for a few seconds Sophie wasn't sure whether she'd heard anything at all, but then suddenly Niccolo was drawing back and she heard him swear in Italian under his breath before spinning round to face the elderly couple now stepping out of the shadows.

Sophie blinked.

Vincenzo de Luca and his lovely, charming wife, Maria. Vincenzo was the head of the Italian family selling to Niccolo. Sophie had spent ages chatting to both of them and one of their sons.

The couple were as family-oriented as Sophie's own parents had been, bursting with pride at the achievements of their boys and eager to show her pictures of their grandchildren.

Their stay on the yacht, just long enough to fine tune the final details of the deal—which she had shrewdly interpreted as making sure that Niccolo was the real deal…an honourable man who treated his staff well and was considerate to all members of the de Luca clan and not simply the ones that held the pens to sign the deeds—would be followed by a huge family holiday in Tuscany.

They couldn't wait.

And now here they were, smiling broadly and moving towards them, and Sophie's heart sank so fast she was surprised she didn't keel over from the impact.

Vincenzo said something to Niccolo in very fast Italian and, picking up minute signs of embarrassment, she noted Niccolo's passing flush before he drew her towards him, hand curled round her waist, just as Maria said, with a little whisper of delight to

Sophie, 'I told my Vincenzo when we went to bed that the two of you were in love. I am a *mamma* and a *nonna* and I can see these things.'

Framed by a halo of moonlight, Sophie could see the sparkle in her dark eyes.

Around her waist, Niccolo's hand felt heavy and deeply intimate.

They had decided to venture to the top deck to see what the view was like, they explained. It was such a lovely evening it felt a shame to let it go to waste.

Sophie's smile had frozen into something she fancied might look reasonably terrifying, and she did her best to relax.

They'd been caught *in flagrante delicto*… Except they hadn't been committing an offence. They had been wrapped around one another on the verge of making love and she knew, in a heartbeat, that Niccolo's arm around her was the gesture of a man acquiescing to a pretence that was necessary. For him, the deal would risk being scuppered because the de Lucas were traditional enough to reconsider what they were on the verge of signing if they got it into their heads that their knight in shining armour was a bounder.

And for her?

She knew how much this deal meant to Niccolo and she cared that he got it. And more than that, she had really liked the elderly couple.

She saw the warm pleasure on their faces to learn

that she and Niccolo were an item and, with an inward sigh of resignation, she nestled a bit closer to Niccolo, playing along with the fiction.

Relief and a certain apprehension filled Niccolo. He had expected her to stiffen against him, not move closer. He had banked on their weird body language being misinterpreted under cover of darkness. The very second he had become aware of the presence of his clients on the deck with them, he had foreseen an awkward situation between himself and Sophie, but here she was, nudging her ballet-dancer-graceful body against his side, laughing and chatting without a care in the world.

It was doing the trick, he thought, but what might be the price for this particular gambit?

Something spontaneous was fast turning into a situation where damage limitation might be needed.

He'd thrown the rulebook out of the window the second he'd met this woman. There hadn't been the usual predictable path that always invariably led to the bedroom. A path where certain ground rules were laid down and parameters put in place.

Yes, he'd confided in her, much to his surprise, but had that been enough to fill her in on the lie of the land? Had she got the big picture? That he was a man who wasn't in it for the long term?

That hand looped through his…was it a sign of

something Sophie felt she might lay claim to? Emotion? Involvement?

She was young and vulnerable and had been through a tough time. If she was searching for someone, might she think that that someone could be him? This game of pretence, generated by Vincenzo and Maria's ill-timed interruption, risked becoming a prelude to all sorts of possibilities which he knew to be out of reach.

He gently detached himself as soon as the group began heading away from the deck and stepped even further away from her to bid goodnight to Vincenzo and Maria, giving them a warm reminder that should they want anything at all they only had to ring the bell inside their suite.

'I should thank you,' he said once they were alone, swerving towards the stunted staircase that spiralled down towards the expansive area where their bedrooms were located.

Sophie didn't pretend to misunderstand. He had paused on the staircase, his hand on the steel banister, to look at her seriously.

She hadn't missed the way he had pulled back from her just as soon as he could.

Had he thought that she might be getting ideas into her head?

'It seemed appropriate,' Sophie said, half smiling although her voice was a shade cooler now. 'You're on the brink of signing your big deal and I know, from having spent the evening with the de Lucas, that they might be the sort of uber-traditional couple to disapprove of you having a romp in the sack with the nanny for a bit of fun—'

'I wouldn't have been quite so basic about it,' Niccolo interrupted.

'It's the truth, isn't it? Aside from that, Niccolo, I happen to really like them. They interrupted us in the middle of something and it would have been awkward and shocking for them were I to try and distance myself from you. It would have reflected badly on both of us.'

She met his dark eyes without flinching and continued, unhurried and calm, which was very much the opposite of what she was feeling inside.

'Just in case you might have got it into your head that that phoney display of affection was in any way *real*, I feel I should set you straight.' It was the last place for a confidence to be shared but the timing felt right. She barely hesitated before carrying on. 'I'll tell you about Scott. In a nutshell, we were in the same social circle for years. You could almost say we grew up together. When my parents were killed and the magnitude of their debts began unravelling, so-called friends were suddenly thin on the ground.' She tilted her head to one side, hoping to read what he was thinking, but his fabulous dark eyes were veiled as he looked at her. 'I couldn't keep up with their lifestyle any longer and I was too busy trying to deal with what life had thrown at me to worry about my disappearing social life. But while everyone else melted away, Scott stuck around. He was a shoulder to cry on and I…I gave in. He was persuasive. He was charming. I also discovered that he was abusive and controlling. He enjoyed making me feel like nothing. He watched every move I made and did his utmost to wrest the few friends I had left away from me. I didn't know what was going on and I was just so worn down from dealing with all the stuff that had happened that I suppose I let things run on for a lot longer than I ever would have in other circumstances. But when he decided that yelling wasn't doing the trick and maybe a smack or two might get through to me more effectively I finally got it together to chuck him out.'

Sophie skipped over the fear and the confusion and then the dismay and disappointment she had felt in herself that she had allowed someone to take over her life and put her in a place where nothing had seemed manageable at all any more.

She didn't explain how terrifying it had felt at the time to have placed her trust in a guy who had used it to try and take over her life. It had been a bit like watching a tornado, only to blink and find that the tornado was upon you and you were at risk of losing everything, including your sanity.

'So,' she said briskly, 'there's no need to be afraid that five minutes pretending to have more than what we actually have is going to go to my head. Believe me, I'm not looking for anything from anyone.' Her voice was hard. 'I was attracted to you and the wine and the moonlight and the atmosphere led us to make a mistake.'

Niccolo raked his fingers through his hair. He was shaken to the core. The thought of any man hitting any woman made him feel physically sick, and the fact that the woman in question was Sophie made him see red.

She was so open and outspoken and funny...

He balled his hands into fists. If the scumbag had been standing in front of him right now, Niccolo didn't know what he would have done. Delivering a nice, long, cold dip in the midnight ocean would have seemed a very good idea.

'Sophie, I'm so sorry.'

'There's nothing to be sorry about,' Sophie said. 'And I didn't tell you about Scott to garner your sympathy. I just wanted you to know that I'm not interested in anything at all.'

'Come to my room,' he murmured. 'This conversation can't stop here.'

'I don't want to come to your room, Niccolo.'

'Why? Are you afraid?'

'I suppose I am, really,' she said with a crooked smile.

'Of what?'

He looked so genuinely shocked that this time Sophie's smile was heartfelt.

'Not you, Niccolo. Don't be an idiot.' Something flashed through her head, as fast as quicksilver: she could never, ever fear anything from this man because, however commitment-phobic he was, there was a deep core of honour running through him. Underneath the harsh exterior, he was *kind*, although she wasn't sure he would want her to bring that to his notice.

Comprehension dawned on his beautiful face. 'You're afraid you might succumb? Give in?'

'Something like that.'

'And would that be such a bad thing?'

'I swore I would never get involved with another man again. Not for a long, long time. Once bitten, twice shy.'

'I am not your ex-lover. In fact, if you ever fancy letting me have his full name, he would find out just how long and how powerful my reach is. I would make sure he spent the remainder of his useless life grovelling on the street for coins.'

'I think Scott just needs therapy,' Sophie said. 'Anyway. Enough of him. I just wish I could warn whoever happens to come after me that he's trouble.'

'Come back to my room.'

'I don't want…complications…' She heard the hesitancy in her voice with alarm. She was riveted by the shadows and the angles of his face, thrown into stark relief by the darkness outside and the intermittent lighting inside.

'Trust me, that's the last thing I want,' Niccolo said gruffly. 'But I feel a need to…to hold you. I want to hold you close, breathe you in, feel your softness against me.'

Sophie laughed and felt a whoosh of inappropriate tenderness steal into her.

'I never saw you for a poet, Niccolo.'

'I'm a man of many surprises. I know you're scared but I won't hurt you. We're on the same page, though perhaps for different reasons. Neither of us wants complications. You've been through hell… maybe it's time you allowed yourself some enjoyment.'

'I'm already enjoying myself…being here…' But his words were enticing. She hadn't enjoyed herself for a long, long time. Was this what she needed? As well as wanted? She was still young. Did she just need to have some fun?

He could be dangerous…something inside was telling her that. But he had laid his cards on the table and however thrillingly, excitingly *dangerous* he seemed, like a huge, burning fire, dazzling in its beauty yet perilous if you got too close, she knew what she wanted in her forever guy, and it wasn't commitment issues.

He was dangerous if he stole your heart, but her heart wasn't up for grabs and enjoyment—pure, undistilled enjoyment—was dizzyingly enticing.

'Besides,' she was peering into an abyss and it made her shiver, 'I look after Annalise...'

'You do,' Niccolo murmured, 'although I'm struggling to see where that fits into the picture. Naturally, we won't be all over one another in public. Nothing will change in connection with you looking after my daughter. I have always protected her, the best I can, from my private life, and nothing will change on that front. And if for the rest of the trip the de Lucas see what they expect to see, then that wouldn't be a problem.'

'You mean, on the face of things, you're still my boss and nothing else? At least insofar as Annalise is concerned, but it's okay for Vincenzo and his family to believe that we're an item?'

'We're adults. Two adults who want one another and are both honest enough to admit it. Neither of us anticipated this, even if my aunt may have...' For a few seconds, Niccolo couldn't help but smile at the thought of Evalina, who had accurately predicted a spark but had certainly been wildly over-optimistic when it came to longer-term predictions. How could she have known that both he and Sophie had their hearts locked away for very different reasons? But here they were and the thought of sleeping with the woman looking up at him with a little frown, chewing over a decision that was, in the great scheme of things, not exactly world-shattering, filled him with a heady sense of euphoria.

'Annalise will be sound asleep, and she knows where I am if she needs to find me. But, trust me, she won't.'

'And I'll return to my room afterwards?'

'I don't tend to spend nights with anyone,' Niccolo admitted. 'That's not how I'm built.'

They were walking now, slowly, Sophie trailing her hand along the smooth walnut of the banister that separated a sumptuous sitting area from a space that was clearly designed for conferences and work, with a long table, upright chairs and USB ports everywhere.

The smell of the ocean filled the air, tangy and salty. Romance all around them, a bubble waiting to be burst, but who cared? This was a magical setting and if she gave in to the magic then it wouldn't be the end of the world, would it?

'You've *never* spent the night with a woman? Apart from your...wife?'

'Don't sound so shocked.' Niccolo was amused by her reaction. 'I have a daughter, and the last thing an impressionable child needs to see is a revolving door filled with women.'

'Revolving door?' Sophie asked with saccharine sarcasm. 'I'm not sure that's something you should be bragging about.'

Niccolo grinned and looked across to her appreciatively, anticipation fizzing inside him.

She wasn't a turn-on because of the way she looked—although no one with eyes in their head could deny that she was sensational...no, she was a turn-on because of who she was, her personality, her absolute willingness to say what was on her mind without thinking that she might offend him.

She didn't obey the usual rules that seemed to keep everyone who dealt with him in check, and he was finding that he liked that.

Annalise was out for the count when they checked in on her.

'It's the ocean air and the hot sun,' Niccolo said as he closed the door to his daughter's cabin. 'Tomorrow, the sea beckons. She'll enjoy swimming in it. It's quite different from a pool.'

Their eyes met and there was a question in his as they stood in the quiet of the spacious living area.

'I should confess that there's no revolving door when it comes to women,' he said seriously. He reached out and curled his finger into a strand of blonde hair and then stroked the side of her face and watched as she caught her breath, nostrils slightly flaring and a soft pink creeping into her cheeks. 'I've made sure to be very selective when it comes to the women I've dated in the past. I may not want commitment, but neither am I the sort of guy who would pick up someone on a Tuesday and replace her on a Friday. I treat women with respect and honesty. They know where they stand with me.'

'I believe you,' Sophie said simply, and he smiled.

'Sure?'

'One hundred per cent. I may not...' She looked away with difficulty, but she was so aware of his finger resting on the side of her face, lightly brushing, that she could scarcely breathe at all. 'I may not be looking for a relationship either, but there's no way I would even contemplate...doing anything with you unless I knew that you were a good guy. I made a huge mistake with Scott, but I was in a bad place,' she continued, speaking her mind aloud, mulling over the surprising realisation that she had spoken more to Niccolo than she had to anyone else about what life had been for her over the past year and a half.

'You were vulnerable,' Niccolo said softly, 'and it was your bad luck that someone was waiting in the wings to take advantage of that, but there are always lessons to be learnt from miserable experiences. You're made stronger by what you went through, not weaker.'

'Thank you.' She smiled wryly. 'You're a philosopher as well as everything else.'

'Everything else?' he teased. His dark eyes were lazy and unflinching. 'You need to be sure that you want to do this, Sophie. Are you?'

Sophie felt a second of giddiness, as though she was looking down a vertiginous drop into a black hole, then she made her mind up and took his hand in hers and kissed it.

'Never more sure of anything in my life.'

The next few minutes passed in a daze. Was this the same Sophie who had been so racked with anxiety and so full of sorrow only weeks before?

How could she be discovering what recovery felt like with this man? In these circumstances?

Was that what made it feel right? Being here?

His suite was bigger than the one she shared with Annalise, a sprawling affair with two outside rooms and a massive bathroom, which she glimpsed as he nudged open the door to his bedroom with his foot. He hadn't switched on any lights. There was no need because moonlight streamed in through the thick panes of glass, carried on a refreshing breeze. Overhead, a fan lazily circled, the only sound in the bedroom aside from the sound of their breathing.

Sophie drew in a sharp breath as he traced the outline of her small breasts pushing against the soft cotton of her blue summer dress.

Very gently he began to ease the dress off, the cotton slippery against her arms, against her ribcage, dropping until it was gathered at her waist, and then he stood back and looked, and in response she unhooked her bra from behind and tossed it on the floor without her hungry eyes ever leaving his face.

Her nipples stiffened as cool air hit them and she tilted her head back and sighed as he swept her off her feet and deposited her on the king-sized bed, from which advantageous position she could look at him through half-closed eyes as he began stripping off.

He was truly a thing of beauty. Moonlight, she thought wryly, became him.

He dumped his shirt on the floor then stepped out of his shorts and her eyes widened. She propped herself up on both elbows and shamelessly stared, and Niccolo grinned back at her.

'I like the reaction.'

He moved towards her, pausing to flip open his wallet and rifle through it, then he joined her on the bed, big and muscular, his nakedness sending a tsunami of want and longing racing through her in a tidal surge.

'Now I get to look.' He tugged the dress all the way off and her briefs were scooped along for the ride as she wriggled free.

She knew that she should have been feeling shy and confused and maybe just a little bit hesitant.

She really wasn't this kind of girl. She'd never had a one-night stand in her life. In fairness, she'd never felt this wild, intense level of *lust* in her life before either. She revelled in her nakedness. His dark eyes, roving over her, made her less inhibited, not more, and she wasn't going to pretend that she wasn't as turned on as he was.

Maybe it was months of sickening anxiety, but she felt a tremendous sense of release as he settled on the mattress alongside her and pushed her hair back to lightly kiss her forehead, her temple, the side of her mouth, his every gesture curiously gentle and tender.

'You're beautiful,' he murmured, half smiling.

'So are you,' Sophie told him truthfully, and he smiled more.

'Your honesty never fails to surprise me. I don't think any woman has ever told me that I'm beautiful.'

He covered her breast with his hand and rolled the pad of his thumb over her nipple, and Sophie's eyes fluttered. She moved and moaned and then gasped when he took her nipple into his mouth and did something wonderful, tugging and sucking at the same time until she couldn't keep still.

One hand curled into his dark hair, even as she arched up so as to intensify the pleasure of his tongue lathing her stiffened nipple while the other hand skittered over his back, tracing muscle and sinew.

His arousal throbbed against her and she parted her legs, feeling the wetness between them, craving more than just his mouth on her breast.

She wanted to feel him moving inside her right this very minute, but he was taking his time.

He moved from one breast to the next, paying the same level of attention to the second as he had to the first, caressing one nipple with his fingers, teasing and tugging while his mouth drove her crazy as he suckled the other.

She was panting as he nuzzled the underside of her small breasts before trailing his tongue lazily along her stomach, pausing only to dip into her belly button before sinking between her thighs. Sophie gave a little squeak of shock but then the pleasure that washed over her as his tongue found the groove between her legs closed her mind down completely.

Sensation replaced thought. He teased her core with his tongue and kept his hands on her inner thighs, keeping them apart as he continued to explore. When he dipped two fingers into her she groaned, and felt the slow build of an orgasm.

She didn't want to come like this.

She wanted him *in* her, filling her up, but that tongue was devastating. She moved against his mouth, loving the twin sensations of her core being stimulated while inside her his fingers were equally erotic, driving her relentlessly to heights she had never dreamt possible.

She drew her knees up and her orgasm, as she spasmed and shuddered against his mouth, was as intense as a runaway train barrelling into her. On and on it went, wave upon wave until she was utterly spent.

She lay like a rag doll for a few seconds, but as she drowsily looked at him, once again drinking in his beauty and power, she could feel her sated body begin to stir again.

She stretched and smiled, looking at him with slanted, contented eyes.

Niccolo stared back at her. He could still taste her on his tongue. He was so turned on that he had to drag his thoughts into safer territory, but that was impossible when she was looking at him the way she was now. Her eyes were dark and amused and satisfied all at the same time and it fuelled a heat in him that made his mouth go dry.

For a few seconds, staring at her with the deep, dark night skies outside and the distant whisper of the ocean, he felt a stab of pure confusion, a feeling of being suddenly out of his depth, then the feeling was gone and he smiled back at her, in charge again.

'Enjoyed that, did you?' he asked in a husky undertone.

'No complaints.' Sophie sighed. She pushed herself up and then knelt so that they were facing one another, and she ran her hands over his shoulders, then along his forearms, curving around to stroke his ribcage and circle his small brown nipples.

'I can't believe I'm being…this person,' she confessed, dipping to kiss his shoulder and then tilting her head to look him straight in the eyes.

'What person is this?'

He manoeuvred them so that they were once again lying down but this time facing one another, their bodies lightly touching.

'You make me feel…a little reckless and very confident about my body.'

'You're a beautiful woman with a body to match. Where's the lack of confidence coming from?'

Sophie laughed a little under her breath. Yes, she knew she was attractive enough but that wasn't a sure-fire path to the sort of extrovert self-assurance most of her peers had possessed. She had missed some of the signposts along the way and had ended up the sort of girl who was happy enough to socialise but given half a chance had always been happier with her head in a book or lazing in the gardens of a National Trust house.

This man somehow made her aware of a side to her she had hitherto ignored.

'Who knows…?' She laughed away the sudden serious moment as she began touching him, emboldened because she could see and feel how turned on he was.

This time, their lovemaking was long and slow. She had hurtled over the edge and now he built her back up again, back to a place where her body was humming and on fire.

He paused only to make sure he was protected,

and then when he at last sank into her she was already so turned on that she climaxed on his first deep thrust and felt a burst of pleasure when he climaxed soon after, arching back, wildly and beautifully out of control.

How much time had passed? It could have been a hundred years. Sophie was energised and felt really alive for the first time in her adult life.

She realised she had no idea what happened next in this scenario, although what she *did* know was that he was a man who never spent a night with a woman; she began edging her way towards the side of the bed, but he stilled her before she could clamber off.

'We're here on this yacht,' he murmured, sitting up in one fluid motion and cupping the nape of her neck as he looked at her with a little smile, 'in the middle of the ocean, and Vincenzo and his family now think we're an item. I wouldn't want to disappoint…'

Sophie was mesmerised by his smile. Yes, here they were, and this was a world away from real life. Reality was a plane flight and several taxis away…

'Just while we're here…' She reached out to stroke his face and was powerless to do anything but obey her body for the very short while they would be on his yacht.

'Just while we're here,' Niccolo agreed. 'I may not have the rule book when it comes to predicting the future, but one thing I do know is that nothing lasts for ever. When we return to London, this will be a dream easily forgotten. You'll be with me for a couple more weeks and then you can return to your life with a lot more peace of mind that your financial woes are ebbing away.' He smiled crookedly.

Sophie looked at him for a few seconds. To jump or not to jump…

She had learnt lessons from Scott, the biggest being that when it came to longevity, she would take her time and go safely, go with the guy who would be her rock.

But she had learnt other lessons along the way… lessons from having to deal with the sudden death of both her parents. Life was short, and tomorrow was, after all, another day easily dealt with…

CHAPTER EIGHT

NICCOLO'S CLIENTS STAYED a further two days, during which time Sophie emerged from the shadows of being Annalise's nanny. She had envisaged, before arriving on his amazing superyacht, that she and Annalise would amuse themselves wherever the action happened *not* to be. Certainly, on day one, reclining on the upper deck, she had happily concluded that that would become the routine over the next four days. While big money was made and deals were finalised over fine wine and fine food, she and Annalise would be out of sight, although not out of mind, because she had, of course, factored in the fact that Niccolo would spend some quality time with his daughter and when he did she, Sophie, would busy herself reading or relaxing in one of the many secluded areas on the yacht. It was certainly big enough for her to find a spot where she could be on her own.

There were a multitude of decks, after all, and no less than three swimming pools!

That had been the plan.

Plans, she discovered, changed. Secret desires, she discovered, changed too. Lusting undercover was quite different when the forbidden became accepted. Over the next couple of days, whilst she occupied Annalise in the mornings, enjoying the run of the yacht, including the child-friendly space which had anything and everything designed to amuse a kid, she was invited to spend time mixing with the guests in the afternoon and in the evenings. It had also become routine for Julia to take over childminding duties from six onwards.

Sophie was guiltily conscious of those lines that had been blurred but she was too wrapped up in a haze of unimaginable excitement to pay much attention.

Whatever Vincenzo's assumptions about their relationship, Niccolo made sure to limit public displays of affection, and so there was a heightened sense of awareness of one another as they socialised under the hot, starry nights, dining informally on exquisite tapas served by his various chefs, with the ocean lazily lapping the sides of the massive yacht.

She would catch his eye and know that he had been looking at her, and even if he wasn't anywhere near her she would feel his dark, brooding gaze as powerful as a physical caress.

And the sex...

Mind-blowing. It was as if her body had finally

realised what it was meant to do, as if her femininity had, at last, been wakened, reminding her that she was still a vibrant young woman, still *alive*.

Strangely, she knew that this person who had emerged in the least likely of circumstances would have thrilled her parents. They would not have wanted her to spend the remainder of her youth wallowing in grief. They would have wanted this adventure for her and knowing that gave her tremendous peace of mind.

She had thrown herself headlong into a situation with a predetermined outcome and she was loving every illicit second of it. Eyes wide open, she was doing what she had never, in a million years, thought she was capable of doing…

She was enjoying a relationship that was going nowhere with a man. Love…commitment…any notion of longevity was absent from what they had and, for someone who had always been conscientious to a fault, good at making sensible decisions, this represented a huge diversion from the norm.

With the last of the guests now gone, Sophie stared out at a blue horizon and slowly accepted that London was a mere two days away, once Niccolo had finalised the last touches to his deal and communicated with various departments within his sprawling organisation on the business of briefing the press.

Today, for the first time, she and Annalise would

not be spending the day together because Niccolo was taking her out for lunch.

'Where?' she'd asked, wondering whether she'd missed some other five-star restaurant nestled in an obscure corner of his fabulous yacht. She didn't think anything could surpass the pleasure of eating perfect food under blue skies, with the salty ocean breeze all around and a horizon that stretched limitlessly into a fine strip of navy where sky and sea seemed to become one.

'It's a surprise,' he had drawled. 'The code is casual dress. Let's refine that…the code is swimwear until such time as it becomes birthday suit…'

So now here she was, and she gave a little yelp when she felt him dip behind her to kiss her shoulder.

She turned around, standing as she did so, and her heart gave that familiar flip-flop and all the thoughts she'd been having skittered through her head and disappeared like water running down a plughole.

'I'm liking the dress code,' Niccolo murmured, holding her at arm's length and inspecting. 'Bright colours suit you.'

'It's the first time I've worn anything bright in a long time,' Sophie admitted. She glanced down at the swirls of orange and yellows in her long, flowing skirt and the pale blue of her sleeveless top. In the canvas bag, one of many beachwear accessories available on the yacht for anyone who might need them, was her black one-piece, her towel and the usual array of suncreams and sunglasses.

Niccolo nodded. She confided easily. Little confidences told with a certain hesitancy which he actually liked and had certainly become accustomed to.

She didn't demand his undivided attention and he figured that that was why she managed to get it so easily because he certainly hadn't been able to keep his eyes off her over the past couple of days, when their relationship had gone from platonic to sexual with the speed of a supersonic rocket.

'Make sure you've got a lot of sunblock.' He tucked some strands of blonde hair behind her ears. 'You're so fair you'll end up looking like a lobster if you're not careful.'

Sophie burst out laughing. 'I appreciate the concern. Not to worry, I've packed enough sunblock to open a small shop.'

Just for a second, Niccolo stilled and frowned, disconcerted by a certain protectiveness that had swept over him and even more taken aback by the shift in atmosphere from sexual banter and teasing to something more unsettlingly...*familiar*. Since when did he do familiar? He had spent years mastering the art of conducting affairs without *familiar* ever becoming part of the package. Maybe it was just his imagination, but he wasn't about to take any chances.

* * *

Have I said something wrong? Sophie wondered.

She'd noted the way he had pulled back, a shadow of withdrawal that had been glaringly obvious to her, and after a few seconds of confusion she rallied fast because of course she knew exactly why the mood had shifted.

A line had been crossed.

The way he had touched her just then, the look in his eyes...there had been amusement and indulgence that had made her squirm with pleasure but had clearly had the opposite effect on him. This was just a bit of time out for him, she thought, whereas for her it was...

Well, what was it?

The voice in her head was more insistent now than it had been previously, and her heart began to beat at a rapid tempo. She cared for him. How had that happened? This was more than just a sexual craving for her. Somewhere along the line, the force of his personality, his intelligence and wit, curious kindness and generosity of spirit had pierced through her defences and got her feeling things she had no right to feel.

Had he sensed that?

Sophie felt a prickly, heated rush of blood to her head as the mortifying possibility that he had sensed something she herself had only now begun to figure out took shape.

And he'd retreated faster than a speeding bullet.

He had made it clear what he wanted from this… liaison. She had agreed because at the time it had seemed a simple equation: fun and adventure with no price to pay afterwards. Months of pent-up misery and anxiety had fuelled a response in her that had been easy to categorise. Very quickly, Sophie knew that she had to make certain decisions. She could retreat or else she could enjoy what they had, knowing that she would be heartbroken when it ended.

Whoever said that life was simple?

She wanted to pack as many memories as she could into the next couple of days, enough to keep her warm at night and to remind her of what it felt like to be *alive* after months of living the life of a zombie. Scott had broken through her misery, but his presence had been toxic.

Niccolo, on the other hand, inappropriate as he was when it came to any sort of forever guy, had somehow managed to go a long way to healing her.

She reckoned that might be just about the last thing he would want to hear, only slightly ahead of *I'd really like what we have to continue…*or *maybe we could see where this takes us…*

'I got sunburned once,' She carried on the conversation, her voice light and unbothered. 'When I was ten. We went to Majorca on holiday and I forgot about the sunblock and, believe me, it's a mistake I'll never make again. How is Annalise? We had breakfast together and I left a few bits and pieces with her to do if she gets bored.'

She began walking away, ignoring any awkwardness and shutting down the thoughts swirling in her head. She felt him fall into step alongside her but she didn't look at him.

'Although,' she continued gaily, 'how on earth could anyone get bored on this yacht? Sun…sea… I guess all that's missing is the sand! She might feel something of an anti-climax when we get back to London, but I have lots of things in store that Annalise and I can do together.' She glanced sideways at him to see that he was staring ahead but no longer frowning.

'That's very diligent of you.' He was smiling when he said that and she relaxed fractionally, eager to pick up the thread and run with it.

'I'm a very diligent person.' There was a smile in her voice now as well. 'It's something to do with dealing with plants,' she confided. 'You can't hurry them along. You have to be patient and wait to see the results of all the effort you put in.' She launched into describing some of the projects she had worked on before her university career had abruptly ended and was still chatting as they made their way down a stunted stairwell to a part of the yacht she had not even glimpsed in passing.

She fell silent. Somehow she had expected…she didn't quite know what. Certainly not a boat within

a boat. Belatedly she spotted two of the crew waiting in the wings, and in a daze she was ushered into
the speedboat, along with two hampers and a Louis
Vuitton canvas bag.

Only as the streamlined boat slid out from the
bowels of the superyacht did she turn to Niccolo
with an awestruck expression.

'Really?' she asked, and he burst out laughing as
he steered the boat away from its mothership, picking up confident speed across the open ocean.

'It's an indulgence, I admit,' he shouted over the
powerful roar of the motor, and for a while Sophie
just stayed completely silent and watched the blur
of scenery whipping past her as she held her face
away from the spray of sea flicking up as the boat
shot through the water.

There was nothing to see and yet there was everything to see. Sea and sky and the pure vastness of
nature took her breath away. She'd always been way
too careful to enjoy going fast in anything, from a
car to the one time she had been persuaded by Scott
into riding pillion on his motorbike, but this…

She'd tied her hair back and she could already feel
it unravelling, whipped around by the force of the
wind against her face.

The speed was an aphrodisiac…not to mention
the sight of him, all bronzed, with his shirt unbut-
toned and his shorts emphasising the length of his
muscular legs.

She gasped as the speedboat began to slow and then the deep navy blue of the ocean gradually gave way to paler, lighter blues, then streaks of bright turquoise blending with dazzling clear green, lapping the shores of a completely deserted cove.

With a tangle of trees and shrubs and bush rising against a steep hill at the back, the cove was clearly accessible only by boat and they seemed to be the only visitors.

'An indulgence...' Sophie said as he killed the engine and expertly anchored the speedboat so that it was just a case of slipping over the side into warm, shallow, stupidly transparent water.

'Haven't done anything with it for too long,' he admitted, helping her out and to the beach and then proceeding, in stages, to transport the hampers to dry land.

Sophie smiled and said teasingly, as she looked all around her, taking everything in, 'That's the problem with toys. Sooner or later they get chucked to one side.'

Niccolo grinned and saluted. 'Yes, ma'am. That's told me.'

He pulled her towards him, and just like that all the doubts that had earlier crowded into her head disappeared and she cleaved her body against his with delight.

He smelled salty.

'This is all ours for the day,' he murmured.

'How do you know? Anyone might decide that this is the perfect spot for a picnic…'

'Oh, any billionaire worth his salt wouldn't dream of intruding on another billionaire's territory. They'd spot my speedboat and head for another private cove…'

He pushed his fingers into her hair, undid what remained of the thick plait and then spread it across her shoulders. Then he turned his attention to the tiny buttons on her top, taking his time.

'Braless.' He groaned. 'You have no idea how much I've been thinking of touching you.' He inched her back and then broke free to delve into the canvas bag, from which he extracted an enormous towel to spread on the ground.

It felt thrilling and wicked to be doing this, Sophie thought, already wet.

He had positioned the towel under a cluster of trees, avoiding direct sunlight. While she lay on the towel to look at him—half naked because she had finished what he had started and had removed her top—she watched as he stripped off, revealing his glorious body in slow motion, bit by gradual bit until she could barely contain her rising excitement.

She propped herself up on her elbows and blushed as he stood over her, towering, his burnished torso roughened with dark hair and his arousal proclaiming that he was as turned on as she was.

He took himself in one hand and idly stroked, and her whole body went up in flames.

Lovemaking in the intimacy of a dark cabin was so different from this…with the warm sun beating down on them and the sea and the icing-sugar-white sand all around.

As his dark eyes skewered her to the spot, Sophie followed his lead…pushing her hands under the soft, tissue-paper-thin skirt and then pressing her fingers against herself until a burst of sensation began spreading through her.

Niccolo smiled. He didn't step towards her. Instead he half nodded, urging her on, and she stroked until she felt the slow, urgent build of her climax.

This was shameless, wanton…but oh, so shockingly erotic. She came in a surge of pleasure, her body quivering and arching against her fingers. In her most intimate moment, this man had seen her and it felt right, somehow.

'Your turn,' she murmured as he sank down next to her on the oversized towel.

He grinned and nibbled the side of her mouth while simultaneously relieving her of her skirt and underwear, out of which she helpfully wriggled without separating from his small kisses. 'You look like a sexy, ruffled little angel. I like it. A lot. And I have more important things to do right now than worry about my own needs…'

'What have you got to do?' Sophie pouted. She

was still warm and tingly as her body gradually began to calm.

By way of response, Niccolo reached across her to her bag, extracted the sunblock and informed her that it was time for him to make sure she was fully protected against the damaging effects of the sun.

'Don't be fooled,' he warned piously as he slapped some cream on the palm of his hand, 'by the fact that we're lying in partial shade. This sun is ferocious. The last thing I want is for you to have to experience a bout of nasty sunburn. Now, where would you like me to start? Front or back?'

It was a luxurious experience. His hands were cool and slippery, and he paid minute attention to every square inch of her body. He rolled his hands over her breasts, cupping them and massaging the cream onto her, then along her waist and over her stomach, and then came her thighs, on the outside… and on the inside, and she whimpered, eyes closed, as he smoothed his hands over the sensitive skin of her inner thighs, nudging her wetness along the way, teasing her just so much but no more.

It was a lazy, sensuous experience and it was clear he was beyond aroused, but instead of taking things further he finished his very thorough job of applying the suncream. Once it was dry, he suggested they should take a dip in the sea.

'Sensible of you to get waterproof sunblock,' he announced, vaulting upright while she hurriedly followed suit, although he stopped her before she could slip into her swimsuit. 'You won't need that. You're fully protected from those harmful UV rays…'

'I had no idea you had a degree in medicine,' Sophie returned, turned on and amused and completely in the moment.

'I'm a man of many talents…' Niccolo grinned wolfishly at her and then casually reached to circle her nipples with his fingers until she was breathing quickly, mouth parted, nostrils flaring just enough to tell him how turned on she could be by the merest touch.

The sea was warm, the water so clear that she could see her nakedness distorted in it, moving this way and that as they swam out, he with long, sure strokes, she following behind and catching up when he stopped to lie on his back, floating.

She joined him in gazing up into the bluest of skies and wondered whether this was the sort of perfection that could be bottled. If it could, then she would make a fortune.

To one side, the speedboat bobbed gently, and as he had said to her there was no one else around. They could have been marooned on a desert island.

She was overwhelmed by a feeling of utter peace and contentment and her thoughts were drifting too sleepily in time to the small ebbs of current under her to focus on anything much bigger than *I'm happy.*

'Penny for them,' Niccolo murmured from next to her.

'I'm offended you think that my thoughts come that cheap,' she said, her smile evident in her voice. Their bodies were touching ever so slightly and each passing touch, with the warm water slapping against them, turned her on. Even through the haze of intense happiness washing over her, Sophie was astute enough to realise that giving him any kind of unedited version of what was *actually* going through her head would be a horrendous mistake. 'I'm thinking that it's a shame the sea back home is way too cold to do anything like this. I could float along and just fall asleep right here. Penny for yours.'

With his own question thrown back at him, Niccolo found himself actually considering what she had asked. What was he thinking?

And just for a second, he was alarmed by the disconcerting realisation that he was thinking that he didn't want this to end. In a life spent in the fast lane, where decisions were made that changed lives and finding time out was always something that had to be worked at, this was relaxation at its most perfect, and he didn't want it to end.

It was a ridiculous thought, of course. Hadn't he lived with a first-hand vision of how life panned out for people who didn't throw everything into work?

Evalina, touring the world until she was a little

too old for the luxury of being a nomad, would have ended up in a pitiful, low-paid job had it not been for him.

His parents, irrespective of their love for one another, had similarly failed to realise the vital importance of putting work first and had ended up vulnerable to the consequences, which had been miserable.

He had built his life on the very simple acceptance of certain unquestionable facts.

You worked hard, you accumulated wealth, and you gained freedom from anyone to have a say over the direction of your life.

So this fleeting notion that relaxing as he was doing right now could possibly have any kind of place in his high-octane life was, frankly, foolish.

But it still unsettled him that he could even think like that.

'I'm thinking,' he drawled, 'that this has been a very successful trip work wise and, as an end to my very satisfying closure on the de Luca deal, a couple of hours here couldn't be better.'

Sophie felt a cool trickle run through her because that was as direct a reminder she could get that what they were enjoying had its limits, boundaries beyond which it would not be allowed to run.

'And,' she pointed out, stung by the fact that she had become way too involved with someone who just wanted a playmate for a few days, 'it's also been great for you and Annalise.'

'Meaning?'

He flipped over, treading water for a few seconds, while his eyes met hers, cool and questioning, and that cold trickle got a tiny bit colder.

But they were lovers and why shouldn't she say what was on her mind? He was only allowed so many ground rules!

It was a mischievous thought but, once lodged in her head, it stubbornly refused to budge.

They were in a bubble where he was no longer her employer and she was no longer his employee. She could revert back to being tactful and discreet when they returned to the UK, just as she would re-vert back to being the woman who no longer had the pleasure of touching the man she never wanted to stop touching.

'You're not really that interested in hearing what I have to say, are you?' She looked at him for a couple of seconds and then forked off, back towards shore, swimming as fast as she could and aware that he was easily gaining on her without much effort.

But she made it back to the beach and stood up, heading straight for one of the towels in the big can-vas bag and wrapping it around herself.

When she turned, it was to see that he had slung a towel round his waist and was moving to the one on the ground, beckoning her to accompany him, his expression no longer cool and remote.

'I'm not used to people being as forthright with me as you are,' Niccolo told her quietly, which, for a moment, rendered her a little speechless because she had expected him to move into defence mode, prepared to guard his precious ivory tower whatever the cost. 'You want to talk to me about Annalise, and of course I want to hear what you have to say. So tell me and don't think that you have to hold back.'

Sophie hazarded a small smile. 'When I first arrived,' she said boldly, 'I would say that the interactions between the two of you were incredibly formal.' She ignored his developing frown and the dark flush spreading across his high cheekbones. He looked *uncomfortable* and her heart went out to him. Ivory towers had definite drawbacks, and not having the privilege of people daring to confront you had to be one of those drawbacks. Perhaps even his aunt and his parents would not go where she was now determined to tread, but then they would be in his life for ever, whereas she was a temporary fixture, soon to be dispatched.

'Formal...like how?'

'I could see how much you love your daughter, Niccolo,' she said gently. 'And it's obvious how hard you work to give her the sort of life you never had, but sometimes I almost got the feeling that you might feel more comfortable if she just saluted you as a greeting instead of running towards you for a hug.'

She watched as he raked his fingers through his hair, and her keen eyes noted that there was just the slightest tremble there, although his expression remained composed and pensive.

'Now,' she said on a deep breath, 'you just seem so much more relaxed around her and I can tell she feels it as well. She lights up when you come into the room. I don't think she really knows that, and you probably don't either, but I see it because I'm perched on the outside and sometimes it's easier to spot stuff as a spectator.'

'I've...yes... I've known it as well...' His voice was gruff. 'I've seen the way Annalise feels more comfortable around me.' He shot her a crooked smile. 'Maybe you have something to do with that.' He shrugged.

'I don't think so,' Sophie returned thoughtfully, then she paused, before adding, 'I won't be around for much longer, so you have to promise me that it's a closeness that's going to last, to get stronger, even.'

Not going to be around for much longer...
Those words penetrated Niccolo's consciousness and he felt a gut-level dismay, which he slammed a lid on fast.

'Scout's honour,' he drawled, putting a full stop under any further heart-to-heart, touchy feely conversation. 'And now…let's park that topic because I can think of a hundred more things I'd rather do…'

'A hundred?'

'Okay, maybe just the one…'

'And what might that be?'

'Lunch, of course.' He grinned and then chuckled. 'What else were you thinking?'

CHAPTER NINE

TWENTY-FOUR HOURS LATER, as she watched him play in the pool with Annalise, Sophie was thinking that time was running out.

The deal had all been concluded three days earlier. It had hit the headlines two days ago and Niccolo had spent time on various calls, some of which were with the financial press, who were asking for details of how he saw the company moving forward.

She knew that because, for once, he had not retired to his dedicated office aboard the yacht to do business but instead had sat at the low glass table on the middle deck where she and Annalise had been spending the day, watching them and joining in when time permitted, only breaking off to take calls, answer emails and communicate with all the people who seemed desperate to have air time with him.

Now there was no further reason for them to remain on the gently floating yacht. Reality was a heartbeat away and it was beckoning.

She didn't want it to. When she thought about the cut and dried business of returning to London, where this moment in time would be forgotten, she felt physically sick.

She had embarked on this brief affair and if there had been a certain apprehension that the water she was stepping into might prove a little deeper than she wanted, she had not expected to find herself in water so deep that she was in danger of drowning.

Stepping back from the past year and a half, she felt she could disentangle all the threads that had wrapped themselves around her in a frightening stranglehold.

She could mourn the loss of her parents and see that although the loss would always be a part of her, the sun would still keep rising and setting and life would still be there, waiting to be lived, which was what her parents would have wanted for her.

And it helped that the fabulous sums of money she was being paid, plus the sale of the family home, actually meant that she no longer had to panic about her finances.

She also knew now that Scott, the guy who had loomed so large and caused her so much grief, had been merely a blip on her confused horizons.

Not because Niccolo had been a pleasant distraction, supplanting those depressing memories with more uplifting ones. Not because he had shown her that she was still capable of having fun, had taken her to a place where she had been able to glimpse sunshine through the dark clouds, but because he had filled her entire world with sunshine. She had been roused, like Sleeping Beauty, except she knew it wasn't going to last.

And it scared her to imagine what life was going to be without him as a physical presence in it.

She was beginning to think that despite what she had told herself about lessons learnt, she was fundamentally a girl who had grown up with the love of parents who had set a shining example of what a happy life should look like. Her faith in love was too strong to be destroyed by one bad experience. Niccolo had shown her that. Unfortunately, he was the wrong guy for her.

As though sensing that her thoughts were on him, he turned to look at her, shielding his eyes from the glare of the sun, and grinned.

'Care to join the fun?' he called and Sophie, also shading her eyes, smiled back at him.

In front of his daughter, he remained her boss and she was the responsible nanny.

Annalise was oblivious to any undercurrents.

'The fun's happening right here, thank you!' She tapped the book which she had not been reading for the past twenty minutes because her mind had been going round and round in circles. 'If I don't finish this before we head back, then I'll never finish it!' she carolled, almost kicking herself for bringing to his attention the inevitability of their imminent departure.

Yet it was a subject that had to be raised and she was already prepping herself to be nonchalant when it was.

She couldn't see his expression when he laughed a response and she actually did force herself to read and to try and relax for the next couple of hours. Annalise, who had endeared every member of staff to her, had her favourite dinner prepared for her by the chef, and then she insisted on going with Julia to the bit of the boat with a glass bottom which gave her a view under the water, even though Sophie laughingly told her that there wouldn't be much to see at night.

Suddenly, the silence left by Annalise's disappearance, the lack of comforting background childish chatter, felt awkward.

Was it because of all the thoughts that had been wreaking havoc in her head? The fact that she was getting to the point where she *needed* him to tell her when they would be leaving if only to give her the chance to work through her emotions as best she could?

The easy familiarity between them failed to reach the mark as he towelled himself dry and strolled towards her, a dark, silhouetted shape in a sky that was already turning from orange to midnight blue.

'You're tense,' Niccolo drawled, dropping into

the chair next to her and staring out at the rapidly darkening horizon. 'Why? Anything going on with your house that I should know about?'

'My house?'

'The sale.' He slanted dark eyes across to her questioningly. 'You said the valuators came to process what furniture was left that you wanted to auction. Did it all go okay?'

'I'd forgotten about that,' Sophie confessed. 'But I haven't heard from them so I'm guessing there were no problems. They'll email me with the amount I can expect.' She sighed. 'It'll all go towards paying off the people my dad owed money to.'

'Tell me,' Niccolo said casually, 'how much money you have left to pay off those pesky people…'

Sophie laughed.

He was funny. It was something that hadn't been apparent when they had first met, when she had written him off as another rich, arrogant guy who thought he could rule the world and everyone in it with a snap of his fingers.

He had a dry, witty sense of humour that never failed to make her smile.

She told him, and then, for the first time, really thanked him for the very generous salary he was paying her.

'You have no idea what it feels like to have some of that financial burden lifted off my shoulders,' she said quietly.

'I know what it's like to have very little. I can only imagine how much worse it has been for you because there was a time when you thought you had a great deal. And you still haven't told me why you're so tense.' His voice dropped to a husky murmur. 'Is that your way of letting me know that a back massage wouldn't go amiss?'

Except, for once, the dark, exciting promise of desires fulfilled between the sheets failed to evoke that complete emptying of her head as it had done before.

'I suppose,' Sophie said, opting for a bit of a half-truth, 'I can't help but think about the fact that my family home is now empty of everything that made it a family home…and some other family will be living in it, filling it up with different memories, rubbing mine out along the way.'

'I'm not sure that's how it works, Sophie.'

'What do you mean?'

'You know what they say about doors shutting and others opening.'

'I'm not as good as you when it comes to moving on,' she ventured a little tautly, then, just in case he got the idea that this was a statement that was leading to something else, something she quite frankly wanted to avoid, she hurried on without pausing for breath. 'When you've talked about your family home, you've always implied that it was a relief when you left it and a relief when you'd made enough money to move your parents out…to make sure you could set them up in style back in Italy.'

'I've said that to you?' Niccolo frowned and shifted so that he was looking at her. 'When?'

'What do you mean *when*?'

'I just don't recall… Well, yes, I do remember telling you a bit about my family…but—'

'Don't worry about it.' Sophie picked up the edge in her voice and wondered whether he did as well. Why, she wondered, did he have to act as though those little morsels of confidences were somehow a crime against humanity?

She knew why. Of course she did.

For most people, sharing was something that was a bonding experience. It was something they did when they actually gave a damn about what the other person thought.

Niccolo had shared stuff in soundbites, and she figured that it was because he'd wanted to give her just enough explanation for her to understand the man he was, a man who had nothing inside to give and was not interested in any sort of relationship that demanded more than what was on offer.

No wonder he was aghast at the thought that he might have told her anything that had been close to his heart.

It would be tough for anything to be close to a heart that wasn't actually there!

'I wasn't,' he said irritably, 'worried about anything. Perhaps my experiences of the place I grew up in aren't rooted in sentimentality.'

'You can be so...*cold*, Niccolo.'

'Show me a successful man who enjoys hugging trees and cries when he sees a pleasant sunset.'

Against her will, Sophie laughed and then told him off for making her laugh, but in a way she was pleased because the atmosphere had been veering into dangerous territory and she had wanted to find a way of pulling back, of reminding herself that she was in it for the moment, to enjoy what remained and not let despair at what would never be tarnish the present.

He pulled her towards him, nearly causing her to topple in her chair, and she laughed again.

'Annalise might come back,' she whispered.

'Julia will settle her. We're here...the stars are in the sky and the ocean is stirring around us. What could be more romantic?'

He kissed her. Long and slow, barely giving her time to surface for air. His tongue moved against hers and Sophie felt dampness between her legs, aching for the sort of release only he was capable of affording her.

'I'm hungry for you...' he whispered hotly into her ear. 'You've been driving me crazy sitting on that lounger pretending to read when you'd rather look at me.'

'You're so full of yourself, Niccolo.'

'Tell me you don't like it.'

'Your ego is as big as your yacht...' But she was laughing softly again and capturing his face between her hands so that she could pepper his cheeks with small, fluttering kisses.

'My yacht's not that big. There are bigger...'

They didn't make love. Both were too aware that they were out in the open and not in a deserted cove on a deserted strip of white sand.

But he pulled her to sit between his legs on the long, wooden deckchair with its deeply padded cushions. She had her back to his stomach and they were both gazing up at a star-studded sky. The breeze was soft and silky and smelled of the salty ocean.

Sophie closed her eyes and let her mind drift off, but not into any dangerous places because she didn't want to ruin the atmosphere.

The silence should have felt odd, but it didn't. It was warm and familiar, and when he spoke, his voice low and pensive, she wasn't surprised that he was speaking from the heart.

He hated heart-to-hearts. He hated opening up. He saw it as a form of weakness because strength was in moving forward, and only looked back if looking back served a purpose.

'I think,' he mused softly, his chin resting on the crown of her head before he sat back and nestled her into the crook of his neck, 'that I was always a little

apprehensive that my marriage had blotted my copy-
book when it came to Annalise. I think perhaps that's
why I've always unconsciously held back when I was
around her. That and a very healthy mistrust of my
ability to handle an infant without dropping her...'

Why had he just said that?

Was it some kind of fatal combination of stars
in the sky and the absolute stillness of the night all
around them?

How could he relentlessly remind himself of the
restrictions of this passing liaison only to ambush his
own good intentions by doing the very one thing he
had sworn to himself he would avoid doing?

It felt as though he was very good at talking the
talk when there was some distance between them,
but in a situation like this, with his arms around
her, feeling her heartbeat and smelling her flowery,
clean aroma, she had a way of bewitching him into
confiding.

'I don't think there's a single new parent who isn't
afraid of accidentally dropping their baby,' she said
lazily. 'Why do you think your marriage affected
your relationship with Annalise?'

'I have no idea how we've ended up having this
conversation.' Niccolo knew exactly how they'd
ended up having this conversation. The woman
had cast a spell over him! He was amused, though,
rather than rattled. His hands drifted underneath her
loose, sleeveless vest to cup her small breasts push-

ing against her swimsuit. He rubbed the pads of his thumbs over her nipples and felt them stiffen through the Lycra. More than anything he wanted to shove both hands underneath that Lycra and feel the coolness of her skin. Even more than that, he wanted to nuzzle that softness, suckle on the taut bulge of her nipples, lick and tease them until she moved against him, out of control and begging to be taken over the edge.

He couldn't wait to get her to bed.

It was astonishing to think how much she still drove him nuts with desire and how much the thought of her still popped into his head when he was least expecting it.

'We've ended up having this conversation because you raised it. Strangely, it does sometimes help to talk about stuff.'

'Never in my experience.'

'You still haven't answered my question.' Sophie clearly wasn't about to let him off the hook. 'Shall I tell you what I think?'

'Not necessary because I'm already regretting having raised the subject in the first place.'

'I think you've been scared that because you failed at your marriage you would fail at parenthood. So even though you adore your daughter, it's felt safer to keep your distance instead of throwing yourself wholeheartedly into the whole bonding thing. Know what else I think?'

'You think too much.'

'I think it's a whole lot easier to hide behind a wall than it is to engage.'

'I engage.' Niccolo slid his hand along her thigh, underneath the flimsy sarong, and Sophie watched the bulge of that hand as it moved closer and closer to nudge the wetness between her legs.

'I'm not talking about sex...' Her voice was an unsteady rasp as he slipped his fingers under the swimsuit, and then slid one finger along her dampened crease.

Nothing fast, nothing urgent...just a steady tempo that first cleared her mind and then catapulted her body towards the inevitable build-up, the heated flush of a spiralling sensation that started low in her pelvis and then invaded every part of her until she could scarcely breathe.

There was no way they would be interrupted, but she knew that even if a member of staff was idiotic enough to interrupt them, nothing would be visible. They would just see the two of them lying together on a deckchair, staring out at the ocean, wreathed in only the silvery slant of a half-moon.

She clutched the arms of the deckchair and closed her eyes as she came on a long, low shudder of utter pleasure, her body rocking gently into his as she orgasmed against his questing finger.

She had to fight to control a moan as he withdrew

his finger and whispered against her hair, 'There. That was me punishing you for thinking too much. Did you enjoy the punishment? I'm guessing that you might have…'

He very neatly straightened the dishevelled sarong and then swore silently under his breath at the vibration of his mobile on the table next to the deckchair.

Sophie immediately gathered herself and sat up.

Work. Sure to be. And between Niccolo and work there could be no blurry lines. Not according to the role she was playing, the girl who was in it for fun and happy to walk away by mutual agreement.

He slid his long legs over the side and walked towards the railing as he answered the phone. He leant against the railing, his back to her, his body language relaxed as he stared out to the dark swells of the ocean, but that body language imperceptibly changed as he carried on talking, about who knew what because she couldn't hear a thing. There was no inflection in his voice that could give her a hint, but something felt weird.

She wondered whether something had gone wrong with the deal but she doubted it. Everything had been signed off and Niccolo, she knew, would have been scrupulous about the details.

He was that kind of guy.

She dragged her eyes away and, sitting upright on the deckchair, she drew her knees up, wrapped her arms around them and rested her chin on them, looking out at the same dark panorama he was looking out upon.

Out of the corner of her eye she couldn't help but watch him, though, and she tensed as he finally straightened and turned, hesitating just fractionally before walking slowly towards her.

When he sat down, his face, all shadows and angles in the diminished light, was serious.

'That was Evalina.'

'What's wrong?' Panic made her lean forward as he sat heavily at the end of the deckchair. 'Is your father all right? Is it bad news?'

'His recuperation has been nothing short of miraculous,' Niccolo assured her, 'to the extent that he and my mother have decided that a cruise somewhere to aid his speedy recovery would be an excellent idea.'

'A cruise? Are they planning on coming to the yacht? Here?'

She squinted into the darkness and looked around, and Niccolo, watching her closely, wondered whether she expected to see his parents lurking with a couple of suitcases behind the teak bar or emerging from under some cushions.

'This isn't quite what they have in mind,' he told her, with a small smile. 'Their idea of a cruise involves many more people around them on a boat five times the size.'

'That's good, isn't it?'

'It's very good. It also means that Evalina will be back in London by tomorrow evening.'

So what happens now?

Niccolo realised that that was a question he had been putting off answering since he had completed his deal.

But now it was a question that demanded an answer.

He didn't want her to go. Was that selfish? It certainly hadn't been part of their deal. Their deal had involved them returning to normality and leaving this wild nonsense behind when they left the yacht. But then again, in that scenario, the abrupt appearance of his aunt had not featured.

When he thought of her leaving, walking away... he felt a sense of loss and emptiness that had never been part of any scenario and he had no time for that.

Niccolo was uncomfortable with the assault of disturbing feelings and emotions that had no place in the cool and collected life he had built for himself, and he was silent for a few seconds, frowning darkly.

Sophie could feel every muscle in her body straining with sudden tension.

He was frowning. Of course he was. Did he imagine that he had been abruptly stuck in the awkward position of having to remind her of the laws they had laid down at the start of this situation?

She had just given herself to him in the most intimate way imaginable and now everything had suddenly changed.

She could feel it.

She blamed herself for being badly prepared for the inevitable, for being a coward and kidding herself that the bubble they were in was something that would pop but not just yet, and so why think too hard about it?

He, certainly, wasn't torn because she hadn't heard him launch into any speeches about continuing what they had, and just the thought of him mentally trying to work out how to tell her that their time was up without her making a fuss was enough to bring her out in a humiliating cold sweat. Maybe he thought that she might be clingy…might want things to carry on. He was rich, he was good-looking and he had the charm of the devil. Those were attributes that would keep many women hanging on for dear life until he prised them away from him and scarpered. Oh, God.

'That's wonderful.' Sophie tried to inject some warmth into her voice but her heart was breaking in two, even though she knew that she was successfully replicating something of a smile. 'Wonderful that your dad is well enough to contemplate going away. It'll do him a world of good. Both your parents. Do you know how long they'll be gone for?'

'How…long?'

'A month? Longer? Where will they be going?

My parents always planned on going on a cruise, but they never got there. Perhaps somewhere along the line, they realised that they would have to count their pennies. I know in the couple of years before… before…well…there were a lot more staycations…' She was babbling, words pouring out of her while her brain furiously computed the road that lay ahead and the direction her life would now be taking her.

'And,' she continued into the lengthening, awkward silence, 'it's brilliant that Evalina will be returning. Annalise will be over the moon.'

'You think?' Niccolo murmured, still frowning and ill at ease in himself. 'She seems to have become very accustomed to having you around…'

'There won't be any point in my staying on, Niccolo,' Sophie said briskly. 'Annalise has got accustomed to me, of course, but there's no job for me with Evalina returning. Of course, I'll see Annalise at the allotment…' Her voice faded away and the smile felt forced. Her jaw was beginning to ache.

'You'll be wondering about the financial side of things, I imagine…'

Was that all he could think about?

Sophie was relieved and offended at the same time. Relieved that he hadn't seen through her overbright voice yet offended that, after everything between them, he could actually think that she was mercenary enough to focus on the money when… when her world felt as though it was collapsing.

'Of course not. I've already been more than generously paid for looking after your daughter. I'm not concerned that I won't have an extra fortnight to earn a bit more.'

'I'm not asking you to leave, Sophie,' Niccolo said gruffly.

He looked at her.

Of course, they were ships passing in the night. This was never going to last beyond their brief time on the yacht. They both knew that. He had been very clear on that point and yet he was taken aback at the alacrity with which she was already, it seemed, mentally packing her bags ready for departure.

More than taken aback.

'What are you asking, in that case?'

For once, faced with a direct question, Niccolo found that he couldn't come up with an equally direct answer.

'My house is big,' he prevaricated, annoyed with himself for not taking the way out that had been handed to him, for not liking the fact that she was just serenely adhering to the ground rules he had laid down. 'Annalise might benefit from your staying on for the allotted time you were hired for. It's hardly your fault that my parents have decided to disappear on a cruise, leaving my aunt no choice but to return to London.'

'I don't think,' Sophie said carefully, 'that my staying on would be a good idea.'

'Why not? Of course, far be it from me to stop you from leaving, but I'm curious.'

'If I were to hang around for the remainder of my time…well, yes, of course things would revert back to where they were before we came here.' Her eyes on him were clear and direct. 'We've been very discreet in front of Annalise but she's a child. If Evalina were around…well, she's astute and it's not beyond the realms of possibility that she would suspect something. And what if she does? Bearing in mind that there's a chance she might have had some matchmaking in her sights?'

'I admit that hadn't occurred to me.'

Niccolo scowled.

So what if she got a whiff that he and Sophie were somehow involved? Would it really be the end of the world?

In fact, would it be so horrific if they continued what had been started? They were both adults! And if Evalina caught on, then she was an adult as well and more than capable of dealing with the fact that he and Sophie were having a fling.

Yes, the very idea went against what they had both signed up to, but all things in life were organic.

If you didn't adapt to change, you got left behind. Life in the fast lane had taught him that. He had come from nothing and had had to work hard and think fast to make things happen the way he wanted them to.

'We could always just let nature take its course,' he drawled in a soft, lazy undertone.

Sophie stiffened. She knew exactly what he was saying and in some ways she wasn't that surprised.

The fling he'd wanted, conducted away from the reality of daily life and with a time limit he could wrap around it so that he could parcel it neatly away when it was over, hadn't reached a natural conclusion as far as he was concerned.

When Sophie thought about it she wondered whether they hadn't already overstayed their time on the yacht, because why else was there any need to be here if the deal was done?

Had he subconsciously prolonged their time here because he'd known that, once they left and returned to London, they would have to walk away from what they'd started?

Maybe that and the fact that possibly for the first time he was moving from being a father to being *a dad*, with all the subtle rewards that brought.

At any rate, those dark, assessing eyes left her in no doubt that he would be very happy for them to carry on sleeping together until such time as he got bored and decided to call it a day.

He would play with her and then discard her and

his life would move on. Had Evalina really thought that she might be the one to change that? Ha!

She'd stuck her head in the sand like an ostrich while she'd been here. She'd held off thinking about the inevitable because enjoying the present had been too seductive.

Well, Fate was giving her a choice and she intended to make the right one.

'I don't think so, Niccolo.' She smiled. 'And you don't have to worry about the fact that I won't be in the job for the length of time I thought I would be. My finances, for the first time in ages, are actually looking pretty healthy and I finally feel I can get things together and see a way forward.' Now her smile was warm and genuine. She would never tell him how she really felt about him, but she *would* tell him *this*. 'You've been more than generous, Niccolo. You'll never know how much I appreciate being given the chance to look after Annalise even though you must have had some doubts about someone who came with practically zero experience of childminding. In a lot of ways, you've helped me so much more than you'll ever know.'

She stood, began collecting her things—bits and pieces that she shoved into the canvas bag she had brought with her to the pool.

There was a chill in the air, and the sea, dark and flat, suddenly struck her as full of foreboding rather than deep with mystery and promise.

She shivered, and when their eyes met she knew that they were both thinking the same thing…

They had made love for the last time.

CHAPTER TEN

NICCOLO SWIVELLED HIS chair at such an angle that he could stare out of the floor-to-ceiling pane of glass that offered the sort of view of London that people usually had to pay to get.

Right now, there was little to see aside from grey skies and the sort of persistent, fine drizzle that would have plunged even the most optimistic person into a slough of despond.

It was a far cry from the wall-to-wall blue skies and sunshine he had enjoyed a fortnight ago when...

Niccolo gave up trying to shut the door on thoughts that had plagued him ever since he had returned to London to pick up where he had left off before his life had decided to do its own thing and take him on a magical mystery tour of places he had never gone before.

This shouldn't be happening because he shouldn't be thinking about a woman who had always been destined to be nothing more than a fleeting visitor in his well-oiled, well-run life. He had never expected to have any sort of fling with Sophie Baxter but, once he had abandoned his half-hearted attempts at resistance and brought her into his bed, guidelines had been laid down, had been agreed. No promises of anything more than a few days of fun.

It was what he did.

It was the man he was.

He had learned lessons from his childhood. Those lessons had been cemented into him, had roots so deep in his soul that not even his marriage could survive the tenacity of their hold on him.

Looking back on Caroline Ferri, so exotic, so refined, so impossibly glamorous, he could see the cracks that had been there, waiting to open up.

Mistakes were always so easy to spot with the benefit of hindsight. He should have known that exotic, refined and impossibly glamorous would eventually equal high-maintenance.

He should have known that any man who worked hard to earn the sort of money that could give him absolute personal freedom—a man like him—would have found the shrill demands of a high-maintenance woman impossible to deal with.

He had been foolish, but even so…that disastrous union had embedded in him the rock-solid conviction that he just wasn't cut out for the sort of sacrifices that had to be made for a relationship to stay the course.

That was something he had happily accepted.

He had his daughter. She would be the recipient of every single luxury extreme wealth could buy.

She would never be patronised by people who thought they were superior to her because they happened to have more in their bank accounts.

She would never feel angry on his behalf because he had not made the most of what he had been born with, because he had found himself in a position where other people called the shots over the direction of his life.

Oh, no.

Work had come first. It had been the engine that had fired up his life for as long as he could remember.

Women were fun and he was very happy to shower them with gifts, but none of them were there to stay the course, and within those boundary lines he had never known anything but pure contentment with the life choices he had made.

Until Sophie Baxter had arrived on the scene.

When had he started questioning the things that had been the cornerstones of his life?

When had he started looking at his relationship with his daughter and seeing that it wasn't enough to ensure that there was nothing she lacked that money could buy?

He was very glad he had, but even so, how was it that he had not noticed the way those firmly held convictions about how he ran his life had begun to unravel, as if a thread had been gently pulled until every weave in the fabric became unstable?

He and Sophie had become lovers and she had made him feel like a horny teenager. She had lain in his arms and he had been loath for her to leave the warmth of his bed. She had smiled at him and he had felt as if there was nothing in the world that wasn't possible.

Nothing.

Not even the chance to love.

Staring out of his office window now, Niccolo closed his eyes and breathed in deeply, steadying his runaway thoughts.

She'd left. She hadn't tried to find any reasons to stay. She'd turned down his offer to hang on to what they had. She had been polite and gentle and firm, and he only now recognised his reaction to her departure for what it had been.

Love.

She'd carved a path through the walls he had built around himself and managed to get right down to the very foundations where, brick by brick, she had somehow dismantled all his defences and he hadn't seen it coming.

He'd been so intent on making sure she got the message that there could be nothing between them but a brief, flickering flame to be snuffed out the second they returned to reality that he had missed all the signs of his own heart disobeying the rules his head had always laid down.

And now here he was. Wondering where she was and what she was doing.

Instead of leaving at the same time, he had remained on his yacht for a further two days, discreetly allowing her time to pack her things and leave. The perfect, thoughtful gentleman.

Was that why he had done that? Or had he subconsciously realised that it would have hurt too much to spend those final hours in her company knowing that she wouldn't be around for much longer?

He cursed under his breath and vaulted out of his chair, moving to the sheet of glass that separated him, cocooned in his magnificent, expensive ivory tower, from the rest of humanity far down below.

How could he have ever accepted that it was normal to remove himself from the things in life that really mattered? Or believed that happiness lay in isolation? That the challenges of meaningful interaction could or should be sidelined?

And where did this onslaught of introspection leave him now?

At a little after seven in the evening, there was a miserable air of dreariness to the wet, grey vista below.

Most of his employees had already left to begin their weekend.

He had absently mulled over the possibility of digging into his metaphorical little black book and finding himself some amusing company but had ditched that idea as fast as it had appeared in his head.

As he had been doing since returning to London, he would stay at home, spend time with Annalise and dodge his aunt's sneaky attempts to find out what he had thought of Sophie.

And what else?

Think of Sophie?

Wonder what she was up to? Had she decided, after the fling she assured him was a one-off because she wasn't that type of girl, to spread her wings and see what else was out there? Would she be spending her Friday evening in a nightclub somewhere while he remained in his ivory tower, brooding?

She was so damned spectacular that she wouldn't be short of admirers if she decided that there was more to life than allotments.

More importantly, Niccolo thought grimly, could he live with himself if he allowed her to walk away without telling her how he felt?

The very notion of sharing his innermost feelings with someone else was so alien to his mental make-up that he almost shook his head in an attempt to clear it.

The very notion, furthermore, of chasing a woman who had walked away from him was even more alien to his mental make-up.

Those were both very valid reasons for putting the

whole sorry episode behind him and moving on, and yet, even as he thought that, he found he was moving towards the leather sofa on which he had earlier dumped his lightweight jacket.

He had the address of the house she had sold, and with that information he would be able to get in touch with the estate agent who had sold it. Whatever security checks they had, he was confident he would be able to bypass them to find out where she had moved. She would be renting somewhere. He had ensured she'd been paid enough to make it possible for her to rent a pretty decent place.

He could have got his PA to do the leg work, but doing it himself felt right, felt like just part of the road he had to travel to reach her, to unburden himself. To tell her what he felt. To open up for the first time in his life, even though opening up would leave him vulnerable.

Thankfully, finding out where she was turned out to be a piece of cake because she was in the very house waiting to be handed over to new owners.

Having discovered this, he headed down to the underground car park and straight to his Porsche, zapping it open on the move and easing out of the slot without giving himself too much time to think about what he was doing. This was a journey with no turning back.

So it was highly likely that she would slam the door in his face.

They'd had some pretty amazing sex, and on reflection he swore there were times when he had sensed *something* in her, something that had alerted him to an attraction that was a lot more than skin deep.

But had he been wrong?

If she'd been interested, wouldn't she have jumped at the chance to continue their relationship once they'd returned to London?

Should he phone to warn her that he would be coming to see her? Would the element of surprise work in his favour?

For the first time in his life, Niccolo really had no idea where he stood and was facing a situation the outcome of which was a complete mystery.

It was unnerving to say the least.

But the alternative was even more unnerving. He had been accused of many things in his life before but never of a lack of courage...

Sophie had no idea why she was still here, in the now almost completely empty family home.

Everything that she wanted to keep had been put into storage and the rest had been given to charity or sold to help pay bills.

Thanks to her brief period of employment and the money she had managed to retrieve from the sale of the house once most of the outstanding debts had been cleared, she was in the black, no longer swimming against the current.

Yet here she was, locked into some kind of apathy, which meant that she still hadn't moved, sleeping in a sleeping bag, caretaking a house that would soon no longer be hers.

It felt peaceful. It felt as though this last remnant of her past was now fortifying her for taking the next step forward and moving on…

Without Niccolo.

She'd left with Annalise a fortnight ago, while he had remained on the yacht to finalise some business in peace and quiet, because peace and quiet would become relics of another age the second he stepped foot into his offices in London.

He'd been politely smiling when he'd told her that, but she wasn't born yesterday. She'd turned down his offer to prolong their little roll in the hay and he'd shrugged it off, but had then been eager to see the back of her. He might have paid lip service in telling her that there was no need for her to rush away because his aunt was back, but actions spoke louder than words and he was clearly keen for her to leave.

He'd said that sleeping together would change nothing and she'd agreed. She would have fun— and God knew, she was due a little—and he would have fun. Two adults having fun, no strings attached, and when the fun was over, they would both revert to the working relationship that had brought them together on his yacht in the first place.

How simple it had sounded at the time.

She wasn't expecting anyone to ring her doorbell. Not at a little after seven in the evening. Her communications had increasingly revolved around her bank manager and his attempts to help with sorting out all the various debts that had been uncovered following the death of her parents.

No one actually came knocking on her door any more and she padded to open it with mild curiosity, assuming it was a cold caller and already mentally rehearsing how she would tell whoever it was that she wasn't interested in whatever they happened to be trying to flog.

The last person she was expecting was Niccolo.

She'd tried so hard to erase him from her head and yet he had continued to invade every corner of her mind, and so, as she stood looking at that tall, striking, dominant and all too familiar figure, she had to blink and wonder whether her feverish thoughts were so all consuming that she was imagining someone who wasn't really there.

But then he spoke, and her eyes widened and her heart raced and her mouth fell open.

'Can I come in?'

'What are you doing here?' She was struggling to breathe and for a few seconds she wondered whether she might be having a panic attack.

'I've come to…to talk to you, Sophie.'

* * *

Staring at her, drinking in the face that had haunted his every waking moment since they had parted company, Niccolo was finding it hard to think straight.

Had he done the right thing in coming here, after all?

He refused to allow self-doubt to establish a foothold even though the look of barely concealed horror on her face was less than welcoming.

Courage was saying what you felt had to be said, he grimly reminded himself. It wasn't about backing away. He'd never backed away from anything in his life before and he wasn't going to start now.

On the other hand, he'd never been in this situation before, had he?

'What about, Niccolo?' Violet eyes narrowed warily on him. 'What do we have to talk about?'

'Nothing I can tell you standing outside your house.' He watched as she hesitated, and took considerable comfort from that. 'Why are you still here?' He peered around her to the now empty property.

'That's none of your business.' Sophie sighed and reluctantly fell back. 'You can come in,' she said quietly, 'but you shouldn't be here, Niccolo. I no longer work for you and I can't imagine what we have to talk about.'

Niccolo swept past her at speed just in case she decided to change her mind. A baring of his soul was going to be painful enough without him being reduced to doing so outside a locked front door.

Buying some time, he gazed around him at the loneliness of a house deprived of everything that made it a home. There was nothing inside and the bare walls told a story of gradual financial decline. He expected she noticed it as well. The paint was tired, the wallpaper in the room he could see through one of the doors was faded and the floorboards were worn and broken at the edges. Doubtless all covered up when the place had been dressed to impress.

'I'm going to be moving out the day after tomorrow,' she said with a hint of defiance. 'Rentals are hard to get hold of in London.'

Niccolo focused on her. There was nowhere to sit.

'There's no furniture.'

'Sold or stored,' Sophie muttered, looking down but still feeling the impact of him on her, strong and tangible and wreaking havoc with her fragile peace of mind. She looked around her and managed to completely avoid looking at him in the process.

'Where are you sleeping?'

'On the floor.'

'Why?'

She shrugged, ashamed to even think that he might see into her head and work out that leaving him had somehow managed to paralyse her.

'It's hard,' she muttered vaguely. When she raised

her eyes it was to find that he had edged closer to her, close enough to mesmerise.

'There's nowhere for us to sit.'

'I hadn't expected any visitors.'

She froze as he reached out to take her hand, and memories shot out of nowhere, memories of those cool fingers touching her, exploring her body. They had held hands on their trip to that deserted cove, when he had whipped her off his yacht onto his speedboat. He had held her hand on the beach and they had walked and talked and she'd felt on top of the world.

Now he led her out of the hallway into the sitting room, then sat on the floor and invited her to do the same.

'You're in your suit.' She hovered and shoved her hands into the pockets of her dungarees.

'I've come straight from work. What I have to say... I didn't want to put it off.'

'What?' A stab of anxiety replaced the panic-attack feeling. 'Are you okay? Is Annalise? Evalina?'

'I'm not great, Sophie.'

'What do you mean?' She urgently leaned forward while her head filled with worst-case scenarios involving terminal illnesses.

He leaned against the wall, drew his knees up and let his hands dangle loosely between them.

'You're scaring me, Niccolo,' she whispered, dropping to sit facing him.

'Am I?'

'Are you ill? Stop playing these word games. I can't stand it.'

'It's taken a lot to come here today and yet I had no choice. Ever since you left me—'

'I didn't *leave* you, Niccolo. I…I…we agreed… that things would stop when we left the yacht and life went back to normal…and Evalina returned a little earlier than expected and so…there was no longer any need for me to stay on.'

'But I wanted you to.' His dark eyes held hers. She refused to yield to a thread of something in his voice that sounded a lot like *hurt*.

'You can't always get what you want.'

'You walked away from me and left me time to realise how much I missed you.'

'Is that what you've come to say?'

He missed her.

Translated, she knew what that meant. He missed her warm, pliable body in bed with him. To Sophie, it sounded very much like a repeat of what he'd asked of her on his yacht. Would she hang around for a bit longer…be his lover for just a bit longer…just until he got bored?

For the man who could have it all, not getting this one thing had been too much for him to handle. Well, that was tough because she was going to give him the same answer now as she had given him then.

'No.'

Not knowing what to do with that unexpected response, Sophie tilted her head to one side and remained silent. Her legs were crossed, yoga style, and she fiddled her fingers restlessly on her lap, unable to drag her eyes away from his sombre, dark-eyed gaze.

'I not only realised I missed you,' Niccolo flushed darkly, his voice so low that she had to lean forward to pick up what he was saying, 'but also realised that somehow, and I don't know how, you managed to get under my skin to the extent that I couldn't deal with the gaping hole you left in my life when you disappeared.' He raised his hand in a gesture to wave aside any interruptions.

Actually, Sophie had no intention of interrupting anything. She was struggling to join the dots, but beneath the surface his expression was telling her everything her mind was bravely trying to ignore.

There was a soft tenderness there that pulled at her heart strings.

'I never planned on sleeping with you. When I saw you for the first time…' He smiled crookedly and looked down, those amazing, lush lashes concealing his expression just for an instant, before he returned his penetrating gaze to her face. 'I immediately realised that my aunt was up to something when she'd decided to send you along for the job. I figured she'd finally decided to start meddling in my private life because she's never been backward in telling me what she thought about it.'

'I was cautious as well,' Sophie reminded him. 'I'd been through enough and had sworn off men, especially good-looking ones with racy private lives.'

'I know. Truth is, my marriage left me with the deep-rooted conviction that love wasn't for me.'

'Love?' Her heart sped up and she could feel a prickle of perspiration film her body.

'You left, and missing you was just the tip of the iceberg. I fell in love with you, Sophie, and I was too blind to recognise any of the symptoms. My goalposts were firmly in place and it never occurred to me that they were capable of being shifted.'

'You fell…*in love*…with *me*?' She plucked at the braid in which she had tied her hair. 'Please don't tease me, Niccolo. You can't get me back into bed by telling me what you think I want to hear.'

'You admit that you want to hear it?'

Sophie blushed, feeling as though she'd been caught in some kind of trap.

'No…' She thought about what he'd just said and her heart did a few more somersaults. Did she want him to stop? Of course, she wasn't going to fall for any smooth talk and casual lies, but his words were like nectar. 'Maybe…' she fudged.

'Which bit do you want me to repeat? The bit where I tell you how hard and fast I fell for you? Or the bit where I say that I've been a blind fool for not seeing what was in front of me?' His voice was soft and serious and thoughtful. 'I can't live without you,

Sophie, and what I'd really like is for you to give me a chance, a chance for us to build a family.'

Which bits did she want him to repeat?

All of them. For ever and in slow motion. Because happiness could not have felt more perfect.

'Really?' was what she said, and he smiled.

'Really. And to prove I'm not stringing you along, which, incidentally, I would never do, I'm going to do something I always swore I would never do again. I'm going to ask you to marry me. So, Sophie, will you wear my ring and spend the rest of your life by my side? Because if you don't then I have no idea what I'll do.'

'Give me a while to think about it…' Sophie smiled. Cloud nine was feeling good. 'I've thought. Yes. Yes, I will. Because I love you now and for ever.'

* * * * *

Loved Hired by the Forbidden Italian*? Then you're sure to enjoy these other stories by Cathy Williams!*

Forbidden Hawaiian Nights
Promoted to the Italian's Fiancée
Claiming His Cinderella Secretary
Desert King's Surprise Love-Child
Consequences of Their Wedding Charade

Available now!

#4013 THE SECRET SHE KEPT IN BOLLYWOOD

Born into Bollywood

by Tara Pammi

Bollywood heiress Anya fiercely protects the secret of the impossible choice she once made. Then she meets magnate Simon. Their connection is instant, yet so is their discovery that his adopted daughter is the child Anya had to give up...

#4014 RECLAIMING HIS RUINED PRINCESS

The Lost Princess Scandal

by Caitlin Crews

When Amalia discovers she's not the crown princess everyone thought she was, retreating to the Spanish island where she once tasted illicit freedom is her only solace. Until she realizes billionaire Joaquin in also in residence—and still devastatingly smoldering...

#4015 A DIAMOND FOR MY FORBIDDEN BRIDE

Rival Billionaire Tycoons

by Jackie Ashenden

Everyone thought I, Valentin Silvera, was dead. I'd faked my death to escape my abusive father. Now I'll reclaim what's mine, including Olivia, my heartless brother's bride! But with a heart as dark as mine, can I offer what she truly deserves?

#4016 A CINDERELLA FOR THE PRINCE'S REVENGE

The Van Ambrose Royals

by Emmy Grayson

Marrying Prince Cass allows bartender Briony to join the royal family she's never known. Their powerful attraction sweetens the deal...but will it still be a fairy tale after Cass admits that making her his bride is part of his revenge plan?

*Bollywood heiress Anya fiercely protects the secret
of the impossible choice she once made. Then she
meets magnate Simon. Their connection is instant,
yet so is the discovery that his adopted daughter is t
he child Anya had to give up...*

*Read on for a sneak preview of
Tara Pammi's next story for Harlequin Presents,*
The Secret She Kept in Bollywood.

It was nothing but absurdity.

Her brothers were behind a closed door not a few hundred
feet away. Her daughter—one she couldn't claim, one she
couldn't hold and touch and love openly, not in this lifetime—
was also behind that same door. The very thought threatened to
bring Anya to her knees again.

And she was dragging a stranger, a man who'd shown her
only kindness, along with her into all this. This reckless woman
wasn't her.

But if she didn't do this, if she didn't take what he offered, if
she didn't grasp this thing between them and hold on to it, it felt
like she'd stay on her knees, raging at a fate she couldn't change,
forever... And Anya refused to be that woman anymore.

It was as if she was walking through one of those fantastical
daydreams she still had sometimes when her anxiety became
too much. The one where she just spun herself into an alternate
world because in actual reality she was nothing but a coward.

Now those realities were merging, and the possibility that she could be more than her grief and guilt and loss was the only thing that kept her standing upright. It took her a minute to find an empty suite, to turn the knob and then lock it behind them.

Silence and almost total darkness cloaked them. A sliver of light from the bathroom showed that it was another expansive suite, and they were standing in the entryway. Anya pressed herself against the door with the man facing her. The commanding bridge of his nose, which seemed to slash through his face with perfect symmetry, the square jaw and the broad shoulders—the faint outline of his strong, masculine features guided her. But those eyes, wide and penetrating, full of an aching pain and naked desire that could span the width of an ocean—she couldn't see those properly anymore. Without meeting those eyes, she could pretend this was a simple case of lust.

Simon, she said in her mind, tasting his name there first. He was so tall and broad that even standing at five-ten she felt so utterly encompassed by him.

Simon, with the kind eyes and the tight mouth and a fleck of gray at his temples. And a banked desire he'd been determined to not let drive him.

But despite that obvious struggle, he was here with her. Ready to give her whatever she wanted from him.

What do I want? How far am I going to take this temporary absurdity?

Don't miss
The Secret She Kept in Bollywood,
available June 2022 wherever
Harlequin Presents books and ebooks are sold.

Harlequin.com